THE
WHITE
CITY

THE WHITE CITY

Translated from the Swedish by Saskia Vogel

KAROLINA RAMQVIST

Black Cat
New York

First published as *Den vita staden* by Norstedts in 2015.

The cost of this translation was defrayed by a subsidy from the Swedish Arts Council, gratefully acknowledged.

First Grove Atlantic paperback edition: February 2017

Published simultaneously in Canada
Printed in the United States of America

FIRST EDITION

ISBN 978-0-8021-2595-8
eISBN 978-0-8021-8987-5

Library of Congress Cataloging-in-Publication Data

Names: Ramqvist, Karolina, 1976- author. | Vogel, Saskia, translator.
Title: The white city / Karolina Ramqvist ; translated from the Swedish by
    Saskia Vogel.
Other titles: Vita staden. English
Description: First edition. | New York : Black Cat, 2017.
Identifiers: LCCN 2016030009 (print) | LCCN 2016032017 (ebook) | ISBN
    9780802125958 (paperback) | ISBN 9780802189875 (eBook)
Subjects: | BISAC: FICTION / Literary.
Classification: LCC PT9877.28.A36 V5813 2017 (print) | LCC PT9877.28.A36
    (ebook) | DDC 839.73/8--dc23
LC record available at https://lccn.loc.gov/2016030009

Black Cat
an imprint of Grove Atlantic
154 West 14th Street
New York, NY 10011

Distributed by Publishers Group West

groveatlantic.com

17 18 19 20   10 9 8 7 6 5 4 3 2 1

THE
WHITE
CITY

I T was the end of winter. Under the sky that had always been there, now dark, the house still looked almost new. It had a sort of shine to it and was surrounded by nothing but silence and snow. Snow framed the large frosted windows and rose from the shadows, piling in high drifts against the walls of the house. Not a shovel had been lifted.

The wind-whipped snow had formed a small drift on the front steps. A frozen wave revealing that no one had come or gone for several days.

The door was bolted shut and secured with several locks from within, and just inside stood a torn paper bag overflowing with white and brown envelopes. Bills and unopened letters. The cold floor was mottled with meltwater and mud splatter, as was the bag.

The hall was dark, as if it weren't morning at all. A dirty mirror hung askew. Karin, barefoot and naked, stood before it, while propping open the door to the bathroom so its light would fall across her body. Her skin was goose-pimpled from the cold, pale and bluish. Her stomach sagged and her breasts were heavy and unshapely. The left one had swelled during the night, and the skin was stretched so thin a web of veins showed through.

S HE PULLED the skin on her belly until it was smooth and leaned forward to study the stretch marks rising in glossy relief from groin to navel. During her last flight to New York, she'd been woken by the pilot's voice on the speakers, suggesting they take in the view over Iceland. She'd sat up and gazed down at the island, which was almost entirely covered by glaciers, and had noticed streaks in the ice. Black rivers spreading out like a giant's mane, thousands of strands running across the frozen ground.

The traces pregnancy had left on her stomach looked just like that. Seeing these marks now, she felt as far away from them as she'd felt from the ice, flying thirty thousand feet above it.

During her pregnancy, she'd convinced herself that if she worried enough about getting stretch marks, she wouldn't get any.

Now she knew that wasn't how it worked.

Fear can't be used like an incantation; it's an unease that wells up when you know what's at stake. It's not true that what you worry about the most isn't going to happen. Rather, it's highly likely that it will.

OUTSIDE ON the lake, plates of ice moved toward each other, in anticipation of freezing into a solid mass. The gray water churned around them in rippling waves. The dark forest rose above the white speckled cliffs on the far shore and the faint outline of a dock could be made out at the bottom of the property, where reeds and brittle blades of grass jutted from mounds of rumpled snow.

The weather had been changeable over the past days, or had it been weeks now? It had grown milder and had even begun to thaw. From her spot on the barstool at the kitchen island—his spot—she'd watched the lake open up like a gray, gaping mouth. Then the chill returned, a kind of paralysis, but the wind blew with such force that the lake couldn't freeze over.

In the bathroom, the fan was switched off, and as soon as she turned the water on, the mirrors fogged, turning the same whitish hue as the ice. Her back was cloaked in steam when she stepped out of the shower, the water still running, and hurried into the hall to check on the baby. She loathed the feeling of the cold, grimy floor against her bare feet. At this time of day, the house was at its most biting.

Dream sat on the living room floor in her diaper, facing away from her, playing with a white iPhone charger. She never seemed to tire of the whipping sound made by the thin metal tip hitting the parquet floor, or of the realization that she was in control: *her* hand was making a fist and *she* was moving the cable.

She stopped to watch the child amusing herself, unaware of the forces that shaped their existence. Their existence, which seemed so hushed, so spent. She hadn't yet been able to grasp that this moment in time was also the start of another person's life.

She took in the chubby body and its irregular, jerky movements. Dream was still something of a mystery to her. Those large, close-set eyes were unfamiliar in a way that made her ill at ease. A lock of hair jutted from the crown of the baby's head. In the middle of each of her puffy cheeks was a chapped, ruddy patch, which she assumed was from the cold, dry air. Through the baby's soft flesh, a perfect spine could be glimpsed.

She knew the child would one day become the most precious thing she had, but until then, it was pure luck that Dream was so calm. Perhaps you didn't get the child you deserved; you got the one you could handle.

She finished her shower with the bathroom door open onto the hall so she could keep an eye on Dream. When she was done, she peered out and saw the little one still sitting there in the living room with her cable. She dried off and slipped into his robe, the only one left after she sold all of her kimonos.

It weighed down her shoulders; it was far too big.

His body had always been red and hot when he'd put it on.

She knotted the belt around her waist, pulled it tight, and leaned against the sink, drinking in the scent of him, which lingered deep in the thick terry cloth. Toothpaste and deodorant and wet, warm male skin.

The promise that everything was going to be okay.

She wished the damp heat wouldn't dissipate so quickly, but it did. And when she stepped out of the bathroom, it was even colder than she'd expected. She'd shut off the underfloor heating throughout the house, so now whenever the slightest wind blew, an icy draft would find its way in.

She should go into the garage, find the duct tape he kept there, and seal the vents by the windows in the big room— oversize panes of tinted bulletproof glass so large they couldn't really be called windows.

But she never got around to it.

Though she was tall, the bathrobe practically dragged on the floor. Her slippers were upstairs. Something was stuck to the sole of her foot and when she wiped it on the terry cloth, it sounded like a small stone falling to the parquet.

DREAM WAS ice-cold. On the sofa lay a onesie that was as good as clean, and as she dressed her in it she tried to rub the warmth back into her legs and feet. She carried the baby through the large open room, into the kitchen, and switched on the kettle. The sink had an odor, an intermittent whiff of rot she'd come to know well.

She put Dream down on the floor next to the barstool, closed her eyes. While the kettle boiled, she focused on her breath, visualizing the movement of water and air and paying attention to the flow of air through her nostrils, first left, then right.

The doorbell chimed.

Fuck.

It chimed again. A synthetic triadic chord.

She hadn't expected the buyer to arrive so soon, but then it hit her: that's just how this goes. They called and said they'd seen the ad and wanted to come take a look right away.

She knew the feeling. She remembered what it was like to covet something.

She picked up Dream and hurried upstairs, took the bag out of the closet, and ran back down to open the door, sweeping aside the bank of snow on the stoop.

Outside, it was gray and windy.

The wind wailed and the cold rushed in, settling in her wet hair, grabbing hold.

On the steps was a woman her age. Baseball cap, fur coat, black rubber riding boots. They greeted each other and shook hands and she made an effort to smile. She shut the door and made the woman stand just inside.

Held up the bag.

"You wanted to see this one, right?"

The woman nodded and said she was going on vacation and this model was so practical for travel, smiled when Dream waved in her direction, and asked if she was on maternity leave.

"Yes."

She managed another smile and held out the bag. Even the lining was in good condition; the subtle pattern brought to mind the patios of expensive restaurants and white sand.

"So, are you selling any others?"

"Yeah, I've got a few. One lovely 2.55 . . . Chanel."

The woman nodded. She scrutinized the bag, complimenting her on how well it had been cared for.

"You know what," she said. "I'll have to get back to you on this."

She lowered her outstretched hand.

"Is it the price?"

"No, that's fine." The woman looked at the bag again. "It's just that I would like a certificate of authenticity validated by the store. It's not that I don't trust you, but if I ever decide to sell it myself, well, you understand. If you can get me one, I'll take it."

The winter air nipped at her as she stood in the doorway, bag in hand, watching as the woman got into her car and set the windshield wipers in motion. A relentless gust pummeled the house and she had to tug with all her might to shut the front door, but the drifting snow still reached her.

She rubbed her feet against her calves; snow and melt dripped down them.

She couldn't bring herself to take the bag upstairs. When she had bolted the door, she hung the bag on a hook in the hall, swore out loud, and went into the kitchen to turn the kettle back on, trying to feel grateful that at least the electricity was still flowing through the wires.

She took out the tea canister and measured out as little as possible. Then she put Dream down on the floor by the sofas, walked to the kettle, and poured the boiling water over the tea leaves, plagued by the thought that she would accidentally spill the hot water on Dream and scald her.

The brochures she'd been given at the pediatrician's office said that most serious accidents with children happen in the home. Boiling water, falls, crush injuries. She could picture it: She'd run into the bathroom with Dream and shower her with cold water. Or would she call an ambulance first? How difficult it would be to do both things at once.

✳︎   ✳︎   ✳︎

Holding her mug, she sat on the barstool at the kitchen island.
His spot. Where he always, always used to sit and read the
newspaper when he was home. The footrest was freezing. She
blew on the tea and warmed her fingers around the mug. This
had also been his: a chipped photo mug, stained by all the coffee and tea that had been drunk from it.

First him, now her.

That picture of Nicholas on the outside. His smile and a
date and the letters "RIP."

She turned on the exhaust fan, lit a cigarette, and felt the
poison spread through her body.

She didn't get the paper anymore. When the bill arrived,
she'd canceled her subscription—had she known what it cost,
she would have done it sooner—and now she missed it.

In front of her lay a mommy magazine her friend Anna,
Peter's girlfriend, had brought over when Dream was a newborn and Peter was working with John. The magazine was
open to an article about a cookbook author and her children.
Every time she read it, the pictures of them laughing and eating steel-cut oatmeal in a large kitchen settled inside her like
cotton. She felt herself being filled, as if she were the one eating the oatmeal, as if she too were a woman like that, a woman
without a care in the world.

She took careful sips of her tea. It hardly tasted of anything,
but all she really wanted was the heat.

She lit another cigarette and looked out at the view.

The sky was gray, as was the water.

It had stopped snowing.

When she admired the nature on the other side of the glass, all the feelings it aroused in her made her feel ridiculous. It wasn't that she wanted to be in it.

She wanted to *be* it.

She envied it.

She wanted to lie on the icy rocks in front of the terrace and stay there until the stones took pity and absorbed her. She wanted to be one with the great, heavy calm that seemed to exist out there. To be one of the bits of gravel in the clefts of the cliff under the snow, or a needle trembling on its sprig when the pines swayed in the wind. The moisture in the air, a snowflake created by the cold and that disappeared along with it. The down on the swans bobbing together on the water through the ice sheets and waves, indifferent to the wind ruffling their feathers and to the chill that had them and everything around them in its clutches.

She wanted the same conditions of existence. She wanted to be as languid and fearless in the face of her own annihilation.

ON THE slope leading to the water, the snow was thick and undisturbed but for the tracks of small birds. The shrub maples close to the house were still blanketed in white. In front of the terrace doors, the snow was melting. Frozen leaves and pine needles that had fallen the year before could be seen through the shallow drifts. She should have cleared all of it away long before the weather turned; and she would have, had she been able to.

Where the deck was bare, the wooden planks were dappled with white droppings from jackdaws that had flown over the house in the fall. At the foot of the large alder lay black twigs and pinecones, and spotlights peeked out from the white like field mice. They no longer lit up the tree at night.

She used to think the spotlights were cameras trained on her, surveilling her every move at home. Of course, now she knew she'd been paranoid, but back then, when the house was at the center of the action, the thought had seemed completely normal.

Now the house was like any other, more or less, and she didn't take care of it as she used to. No one took care of it. The surfaces—that polished luster she'd once adored—were caked in dust and dirt. Grease spots were simply abandoned. A pattern of coffee cup rings was spreading across the kitchen island. Dust had collected on the floor, and the large windows were covered in smears that looked like a chalk drawing. Layer upon layer of sticky handprints coated the glass at the bottom.

It had been over six months now.

The growing child was a constant reminder.

The passage of time reminded her of everything she'd wanted, her dreams of their life together.

She should have taken her things and the kid and moved away long ago, but she hadn't been able to bring herself to leave. The house was a part of him and as long as she was within its walls it was as if nothing had happened. Here she could still feel his presence. Sometimes she caught his lanky, broad-shouldered figure out of the corner of her eye as she moved through the rooms.

But each time she left the house, it was all too clear. There was nothing out there. Whenever she approached the front door it was as though she were in a deep valley, making her way through a ravine, impossible to scale, without any idea of what lay ahead.

Therese had moved in right after it had happened. She'd stayed with her and Dream until Alex decided it was enough already and picked her up. He threw her things into his large car, dragged her out of the house, and made her go home. But she had still come back. Either she or Anna had, one or both of them.

They would visit almost every day.

They cleaned and took care of things, they brought food she couldn't eat and films she couldn't bear to watch and went for walks with the stroller so she could get some sleep.

And then it came to an end.

They didn't call her and she didn't call them either. At the time, it had mostly felt like a relief.

They drifted apart and the idea that they were supposed to be a family—an even more tolerant family than the one she was born into—dissolved more quickly than she had expected. It happened so fast she hadn't had time to process it. Anna and Therese said that *she* had abandoned *them.* But they'd probably never cared about her in the first place and had been friends with her only because of John. Because he'd had the last say about everything and everyone in their little world, and because being near him felt like basking in the sun.

Everyone wanted to get close to him.

When he disappeared, she'd thought their circle had been broken, but now she knew better. She was the only one who had ended up on the outside, alone. The others carried on as usual, just without them. They were two stones that had fallen out of a wall and the wall had sealed itself up again.

The humiliation of having been abandoned by the group and the sorrow that had arrived in John's absence drove her deeper into isolation. With the newborn permanently attached to her body, she was ushered into a world of crying and night waking and clear, runny discharge seeping out of her, forcing her to wear thick pads.

She looked at the low ceiling of snow clouds gathering over the lake and cliffs and the black forest on the other side. She looked for tears in the cloud cover, for rays of light shining through, precipitation, anything. As if the sky beyond the clouds was supposed to come to grips with her situation and signal that it was time.

Time to come out of hibernation.

She heard shuffling, turned around, and saw Dream on the floor, wriggling across the parquet as she'd just learned to do. Pushing off with her elbows, legs dragging behind, gaze fixed in the near distance, and drool dangling from her mouth.

Each time she saw her commando-crawl like a soldier in basic training, she tried not to think about how he would have laughed, about his laughter and what his face would look like while he was laughing.

She was the only witness.

Dream waggled along without looking up and seemed to think she could keep on going right up the metal leg of the tall stool. She lifted her off the ground and when she had her standing on her lap, Dream looked into her eyes and laughed.

Something white was in her mouth.

She stuck her finger in and felt around.

A freshly cut tooth. There it was, like a tack in the wet softness.

New things always arrived without warning, and then they were a given, as if it had never been any different. A laugh, a look, a faltering step. Dream's many facial expressions were a language unto themselves. The noises she made with her mouth from one day to the next.

It was impossible to imagine her growing up—that her tiny mouth would be used for everything she'd used her own mouth for. Saying all the words she'd already said and many more that were as yet inconceivable.

HER FATIGUE was bright and jagged. It rained down on her, dispersing her thoughts until they were but white noise. She had no idea how long she'd slept last night.

Her eyes were dry, itching and burning.

A shiver overtook her.

Dream played with the slim white cable, and she sat slumped over the kitchen island, either reading the mommy magazine or staring out the window. She was reading the only piece she hadn't read yet: an interview with a TV host about her struggle with postpartum depression. As she read, she smoked a cigarette and her mind became pleasantly empty.

Time passed in this way for a while. Dream sat on the floor with the cable; dropped it; looked at it with suspicion, as if she couldn't figure out what it was doing in her hand in the first place; and then scooted off. When she reached the sofa, she managed to pull herself to her feet and take a few steps back and forth along the coffee table with both hands on the top. And then she let go, laughing as she plopped to the ground, butt first. She got up and did it again and again, until she set her sights on the charger and crawled back to it.

Her somewhat oversize behind was perfect for this game—a sturdy seat for the little body sitting on the floor. Her back was straight. Her legs were outstretched and open, and once again the cable was dancing between them in time with her moving hand.

When she checked the clock on her phone, an hour had passed. She got out of the chair and picked up the child.

The wind had quieted.

Beyond the window, everything was still but for a seabird cleaving the sky as it dived toward the lake. She stood there holding Dream, the child's hand on her arm, and tracked the bird. Then she put her on the sofa and unknotted her robe, took hold of her breasts and weighed them in her hands to see which was heavier. She lay down and gently rearranged Dream, stuffing the robe under the baby's body, moving her soft alabaster arm out of the way. With a jerk, she scooched to one side so her breast was right in front of the baby's face.

The maneuver was exhausting.

Dream opened her eyes, wrinkled her nose, and opened her mouth wide. She looked like a young predator, shaking her head and hurling herself at the breast, stretching her lips like a suction cup and latching on.

It didn't hurt, but she was overwhelmed by the memory of how the first few times had felt—like someone rooting around inside her with an iron pipe. The pain spreading like chaos. He had lain beside her and wiped the tears away with his rough fingers, comforting her and repeating what the nurse had said: the first time you breast-feed, the uterus contracts to protect itself, and it's supposed to hurt. That was nature's way.

And she'd thought that surely he'd known worse pain.

T HE HOUSE was silent but the constant din in her ears was getting louder—a ringing somewhere deep inside her head, a faint tone that grew stronger the more she tried to ignore it.

"There, there," she said to Dream just to break the silence, and the child replied with the rhythmic sound of nursing.

Dream seemed to enjoy her body's milk in a way that made her wonder if she'd ever enjoyed anything as much. To connect with that intensity, she slid the tip of her index finger between those little lips and broke the vacuum seal between the child's mouth and her breast. The seal was so strong that the baby could hold on to her with only her mouth if necessary. She pushed her finger in farther and her nipple slipped out. It was elongated, like a teat. Then it returned to its usual round shape. It was incomprehensible that such a sensitive part of her body could endure such strong suction.

She put one arm over the baby, who had gone back to nursing, and rested her head on the other, trying to unwind and sink into the sofa. She focused on her body, one part at a time; she noticed her teeth clenching and opened her mouth all the way. Opening and shutting it and working her jaw from side to side to relieve the tension.

She pulled her knees up. Felt Dream's smooth, cold feet against her thighs and thought about her soft skin.

Tried to relax her shoulders.

Dream downed the milk, swallowing while nuzzled into her white breast. Round as the baby's cheeks and head, round as the areola that peeked out because Dream hadn't gotten a proper grip on her nipple again. Round and round, rounds and rounds. The milk dribbled out of the baby's mouth and ran down her breast, leaving a sticky trail on her skin and a wet stain on her robe.

Does the body keep producing breast milk after death? If something were to happen to her, if she choked or a blood vessel burst in her brain or if someone were to break in and take her out for good, it would probably be a while before anyone would miss her. But if she had enough milk in her breasts, then Dream might have a chance of surviving until someone showed up.

She tried to concentrate on the softness.

She focused on what the pillow felt like against her cheek and visualized her breath as waves washing over a beach. Eventually her eyes closed; she opened them reluctantly. She couldn't help gazing at Dream. Her chest rising and falling in the onesie, its fabric so soft, and the skin it covered even softer.

She let herself drift off.

✵　✵　✵

Hunger woke her. Sweat had pooled in Dream's neck folds and had made her hair curl. Even though it was so cold, the child was hot.

But she was freezing.

She seemed to have only enough body heat to keep Dream warm while they slept under the blanket.

Trying not to wake Dream, she slipped out of the robe and sneaked off. She went to her computer, which was connected to the neighbor's Wi-Fi, and placed an order. Then she sat on the sofa and waited, looking at the sleeping baby who was anchoring her here.

He'd been the one who'd wanted to have kids.

He'd been the one who'd wanted to have kids. He had whispered his wishes in her ear. Suggesting a new direction for them, an opportunity. Word after word, long descriptions of how he loved her and what it would be like to have another one of her, who was also one of him.

For him, the idea of a child was a window opening; for her it was one closing. She thought of all the women she'd seen stand before their men, holding out their children and pleading for them to change their ways. She could see herself worrying even more and thought of the family rooms in prisons: the toys you brought, the stacks of coarse, gray paper napkins.

The paper plates.

But after a while, a response to his desire came from deep inside her. As if something in her suddenly understood and also wanted it. Hot, yearning to be touched by his words.

She'd immediately buried the feeling of having been convinced to do this. But now that he wasn't around anymore and she didn't need to keep her feelings about him in check, this particular one had wormed its way to the surface.

Now that he was gone, she could admit to feelings other than the fear of losing him in one of the many ways she'd been warned of. She used to have other thoughts about him too—fantasies about how things would change, the freedom she'd know if he weren't around.

Now he was gone, but she hadn't found freedom. He'd left her without letting go. A new version of him had latched onto her body.

T HE KNOCKING was cautious. It was the kind of knock you use when you don't want to disturb a child who might be asleep.

She was surprised that so much time had passed. Maybe she'd fallen asleep. She hadn't heard the moped arrive.

She got up, wrapped herself in the blanket. Her breasts had almost evened out in size, but they were still strange, grotesque.

She walked to the hall.

There was fresh snow outside. When she opened the front door, it cut a sharp arc through the snow and a warm smell hit her. He was wearing that baseball cap emblazoned with the company logo. His chest was flat and wide.

He must have unbuttoned his jacket just before knocking. He smiled at her.

Without a word, she took the box—hot and moist on the underside—and carried it to the kitchen island. She took a hundred-kronor bill from the drawer where she kept her money—what little was left—her gun, and the ammunition stored in boxes or in freezer bags sealed with colorful clips. And then she stopped herself and took out a five-hundred-kronor bill instead.

Back in the entryway, he'd closed the door and had taken off his gloves and jacket. He looked at her with a sort of giddy anticipation that made her feel embarrassed for him.

She handed him the cash.

"Your money's no good here," he said.

"Really?"

She lowered her head a bit and looked up at him when she said that.

"Yes, really. Of course."

She returned to the kitchen and put the money in the drawer. He took off his boots. Muddy pools formed beneath them. Hung his hat on top of his jacket. His hair shot up from his head, thick and blond.

She heard his heart beating.

He walked toward her.

His eyes were on the blanket she was clutching around her. He took hold of her. A light started blinking on the radio he'd left hanging from his jacket pocket and an order was called in. A distant voice wedged itself between them. He let go of her, turned around, grabbed the radio, pressed a button, and silenced it.

She glanced at his shoulders and arms.

"I guess I don't have time for a visit today," he said. "Gotta hit the road."

She nodded.

He looked at her, at the blanket, and smiled and hugged her before he left, rocking her briefly, like a dancer. She was unsettled by his gaze and his smile, by the fact that he didn't seem to understand what was going on or care who she was.

Without looking him in the eyes, she said goodbye and locked both locks and bolted the door.

In the kitchen, she listened to him drive away.

She ate quickly. Tearing off slices of pizza, folding them and biting down, lapping up the hot strings of cheese that stuck to her chin. Wiped her face with the back of her hand and wiped that hand on the cardboard lid. Licked glistening grease from her fingers, shut the box, and added it to the growing stack.

S HE LAY on the sofa with Dream. The sky was heavy and the air was too; it felt as thick as fog. She didn't know how many days had gone by since she'd last gone outside.

She pushed the blanket and robe to one side and positioned herself so her nipple nudged Dream's round cheek. Eyes closed, she opened wide and turned her head, taking the breast in her mouth and pressing her tiny hand against it so it would empty more quickly.

Gingerly, she touched the child's head.

Her hair was shiny and wavy. It was almost as brown as John's and the cradle cap covering her scalp made it look even darker. She ran her finger over the silky hair and the fontanelle, frightened by the emptiness under the thin skin and what it revealed about the fragility of a baby and the body's architecture.

After Dream had been squeezed out of her, she'd lost her voice for hours. Because they couldn't give her an epidural, she'd screamed almost the entire time. Her voice never fully recovered, but she wasn't reminded of its hoarseness too often because she spent most of her time alone and didn't talk to Dream as much as she suspected she should. At the pediatrician's office, they'd had plenty to say about that.

✳   ✳   ✳

Her genitals still felt foreign. When she urinated, her pee streamed in three directions. They said it was because it had happened so quickly. The tissue had torn, making room for the baby. Giving birth was like being sucked into a storm. The act had taken her body and her consciousness and cut her off from the universe. Nothing in that moment was as clear to her as the fact that the torment she was feeling was coming from within; even so, she had tried to get out of its way.

She'd thought she was going to die.

It was probably the only time she'd actually believed she would. Yet behind this thought was another: this isn't how women die here.

But the pain was also pleasurable and afterward that was all she could really remember. The wild flutter in her lower body, a hot wave buckling her legs, her hips rolling of their own accord. How she longed for that feeling now, to be carried away by a power greater than herself. To become an ice crystal in stormy weather, a bubble on the gray lake where the ice had melted.

There was a twinge in the other breast and white streams of milk shot out, so thin they were almost invisible. She pressed on her nipple and the milk streamed against her palm, sticky sweet.

She looked up at the ceiling and tried to distract herself so the milk ejection reflex would subside. When it did, she wiped her hand on the robe and pulled the blanket over her breast.

She was supposed to keep it warm to prevent engorgement and to keep the breast abscess from returning, but she didn't know if that was working.

She reached for her headphones and her MP3 player, which had been shoved under a sofa cushion. She put on the headphones and shuffled to "Warm Winds" and then to "Deep Sea Meditation," shut her eyes, and let the tones rock her away to an undersea world where every sound was distant and light filtered through heavy bodies of water.

S HE WOKE up when she felt something sticky and warm, maybe blood. She raised her hands and accidentally smeared it on the sofa.

It got on her thighs.

She opened her eyes properly.

Everything was covered in shit.

Dream was crying.

The sky was unchanged.

She tried to get up without touching anything. She shook her head, tried to push her hair behind her ear with her shoulder, and walked, naked and shivering, to the bathroom, where she managed to turn on the faucet with one outstretched pinkie. She shoved her hand under the stream of water and let it rinse off the mess.

The water washed it down the drain. She tried to clean her legs with only one wet wipe and used another on the sofa.

In the mirror, she noticed a dab of poop on her collarbone. She wiped it off, tossed the napkin, washed her hands again, and fetched a wet rag, which she wrung out on the stained upholstery. Then she used another wipe.

The cries had given way to screams that cut through the cold room. Dream lay on the soiled robe, flailing her arms and legs like an insect. Poop was spread all the way up to her shoulders. As soon as she'd been picked up, she quieted down. The child's breath was warm against her neck as she climbed the stairs. A hot stream of air, flickering in the encompassing cold.

She'd moved the changing table into his bathroom, which was connected to the upstairs bedroom. There she was again, undoing Dream's leaky diaper, throwing it out, washing her, and watching excrement slip down the drain.

John's shaving set was still in the bathroom cabinet and his pills and meds were still in the drawer by the sink. A jumble of Zantac, Xanax, Cipramil, Cipralex, and Valium. Caffeine tablets and Viagra. Once she overheard Anna and Therese talking when they thought she was asleep, bickering over whether or not they should take the pills with them. That was when they still worried about her.

Dream was clean and dry and calm.

She laid her on the changing table, leaned over and kissed her belly. It was like pressing her nose and lips into cool dough. She held the soft baby ankles between her fingers, comparing her skin and Dream's; she spread the fatty folds on the inside of her thighs and dried her there. She blew on her and a mild sour smell wafted up.

Dream laughed. Her eyes were light gray but they might yet turn brown, like his. It wasn't clear which way they'd go.

She took the bottle of baby oil from the sink, unscrewed the top, and poured a few drops into her hand. She massaged the oil into Dream's scalp, took out a white plastic fine-tooth comb, and carefully picked off the flakes, pulling the waxy clumps along her thin strands of hair. Underneath, new skin was revealed. It looked so delicate she was afraid it would get scratched if she as much as grazed it with the comb's teeth.

Something about this act made her mouth water as she picked off the rest of the coating, leaving the scalp clean. Dream seemed to like it too; she looked straight ahead and made no protest.

When she was done, she put the comb in the sink and turned on the faucet. She adjusted the temperature, wet Dream's hair with the tepid water, and washed it. Afterward, she took out a soft towel and dried her hair and those small shoulders and that back, which was covered with dark and downy fuzz, like a baby animal's. It had been even thicker when she was newborn; then her skin was loose and folded around her little body.

She put Dream back on the changing table and lifted her legs, holding her ankles with one hand and patting her on the butt with the other. Making a conscious effort to enjoy the softness of her skin—how smooth it was and the fact that she was here, feeling it—she let her palm linger on those tiny cold cheeks dotted with dimples.

Everyone had told her: *Whatever you do, try to enjoy this time. Try to enjoy it, in spite of everything.*

She fastened the diaper and accidentally caught her reflection in the mirror.

Misery.

The doorbell rang.

Her heart pounded.

The house was so big.

The front door was so far away.

She took Dream and the baby clung to her. Her grasping reflex was still strong and her grip tightened as she walked with her through the bedroom, hurrying across the dusky lavender carpeting, rough and filthy underfoot, and down the stairs.

The doorbell rang again.

She'd kept meaning to reprogram the chime, but she'd never gotten around to it and now she couldn't find the instructions, not for the bell, not for the robotic vacuum cleaner or the digital projector. She'd never bothered to learn how to use those things.

He had come back. She noticed how happy this made her. Yes, that was the feeling: a sort of eagerness that could be called happiness. Who he was didn't fucking matter, neither did his embarrassing puppyish behavior.

She put her robe back on and rushed through the room and out into the hall. Not caring about the dirt and gravel stuck to her feet, barely registering the icy floor.

It felt strange to suddenly want something.

She flung open the door.

It wasn't him.

Two people were standing on the steps. A man and a woman. The woman—bony and tall, her face already red with cold—had been here before.

"Hello, Karin," she said, and moved closer to the doorway. When she opened her mouth, a chipped front tooth peeked out. She'd noticed it the first time she had stopped by; it was one of those things a normal person would have fixed right away. The man standing behind her was fogging his glasses with each breath. Both were wearing winter jackets with large hoods. Their compact car was parked in the driveway.

She didn't say a word.

Her cheeks flamed with an unwelcome blush.

She fought the urge to slam the door in their faces.

"May we come in?" the woman said, and lowered her eyes, as if the imposition truly pained her, because she had so much respect for personal privacy.

They used a certain tone, as if they didn't quite believe you understood them, and employed a false, ingratiating manner. You had to be sure not to fall for it. She wondered where they'd learned it, or if only people who were naturals—promising actors like these two—found work in this field.

Dream drooled on her wrist, and she noticed that she was holding her out like a shield.

The woman took another step forward.

The man stayed on the stairs. He removed his glasses and wiped them with a cloth.

The woman glanced expectantly at her colleague, and then at her. "May we come in for a chat, Karin?"

She mumbled something in reply, pushed open the door, watched herself step aside and grant them entry.

Their jackets rustled.

They hung them on the hooks above the paper bag stuffed with mail, letters they or someone they worked with had probably signed. Neither of them seemed to notice it. They took off their shoes, exposing their socks; his had a hole by one big toe.

And then they moved deeper inside the house.

With quiet purpose. Greedily.

Even if this was a purely routine call, they approached their plunder with an ill-concealed, smoldering excitement. They stared in hot silence through her dirty windows, drinking in the view. Her view. They turned around and stared at the fireplace; its little white remote control was on the coffee table even though the gas had run out and it could no longer be lit. They looked at the painting on the far wall, her painting, the one she'd assumed was stolen when John gave it to her.

They had already sent around an appraiser, who'd gone through everything.

She watched them.

"Do you mind if we sit here?" the woman asked, holding a backpack that bore the logo of the Swedish Economic Crime Authority.

She nodded and tried to collect herself, gather her thoughts.

They sat down on the same sofa.

She heard herself ask if they wanted coffee.

Struggling to sound neutral. Polite, but not overly so.

"Sure," the woman said, surprised. "Why not?" She paused. Swallowed.

"That would be lovely," she continued. "If it's no trouble."

The woman looked at Dream, who was sitting on the floor with the cable.

She shook her head and wearily echoed the woman's words, in a tone bordering on snide that she knew she had to temper. "No, it's no trouble at all."

She didn't want to seem defiant. She didn't want to show that what they said or did affected her in any way. She was supposed to be indifferent.

As cold as the icy slurry outside.

She turned on the coffee machine, which she'd filled with the last of his coffee beans just a few days before, and the sound of it drowned out everything else. She brewed two cups, relieved neither of them asked for milk because she didn't have any and hadn't for a long time, relieved that they'd stopped nosing around. But now their eyes were on her.

The gray light made their contours dark and shadowy.

She couldn't believe they were here.

She rummaged in the kitchen and found a package of cookies that had been in the cupboard since whenever Anna had brought them over. She arranged them on a Japanese dish and put the dish and the mugs on a tray, which she carried over and placed on the coffee table. Even though she saw that they saw the perfection in this act, their presence made her feel like a child.

She'd moved around the kitchen as if it weren't really hers, and they'd tracked her every move.

She should probably get dressed, but screw it. Her fucking robe, his robe, this dirty robe where traces of his skin mingled with her breast milk and their daughter's feces, had cost more than everything they were wearing put together.

But they knew that.

They knew about each one of her possessions. Perhaps not these two, specifically, but someone somewhere knew. They had tabs on every last krona.

Everything had been documented, every one of her purchases, each step she'd taken, or so it seemed. Pictures of her on airplanes and at the watchmaker's shop. Tickets to Thailand and Brazil, gym memberships, dermatologists, timepieces, jewelry, cars, boats. The dog and the horse each had its own column.

They were worse than the cops.

They *were* the cops, John had said. The police, the Enforcement Authority, the Tax Agency, the Social Insurance Agency, the Economic Crime Authority, the Prosecution Authority, Customs, the Migration Agency. The government agencies all worked together and shared information about the people on the list.

When he had realized he was one of those people, he'd read everything he could get his hands on about civil forfeiture, and she waited for him to say, *It's only money. They can take what they want; there's more on the way.*

But he never did.

The woman stirred her coffee with a spoon.

"Karin, sit down," she said.

She sat on the sofa across from them.

The man reached for a cookie, stuffed it into his mouth, and then licked the crumbs off his lips. She could hear him chewing and swallowing, and the scent of coffee tore into her. She should have sat down to begin with, shouldn't have allowed them to see that she didn't want to sit.

To get the words out, she cleared her throat.

"What's this about?" she said.

"You know very well what this is about. We're here about the distraint of goods."

The woman gave her a worried look and pulled a plastic folder from her backpack. She slipped a page out and handed it to her.

She took it.

Looked at Dream and her cable and then at the paper, even though she didn't want to.

And put it on the table.

Using two fingers, the woman pushed it closer to her.

"Has an opportunity arisen for you to pay off your debts?" she asked.

"I don't have any debts."

The woman stared at her.

"Well, yes, in fact you do. Since this investigation was carried out, we've determined that you do. This here is your debt to the Tax Agency, which has been given to us for collection. This you already know." She wiped a drop of coffee from her mouth. "After the investigation was concluded, you were informed of the outcome and we've since called and sent letters . . . We've tried to reach you. And, of course, this isn't my first visit."

The woman paused. When she opened her mouth again, she sounded more sympathetic.

"And because we've spoken before, I wanted to come by in person, before the eviction, to make sure you're clear on what's about to happen."

"Sure."

It was all she could say.

She could hear herself breathing.

A sparrow landed on the terrace railing.

It pecked at the wood.

The woman's eyes were wide open, compassionate.

"The assets will be seized in order to cover your outstanding tax debt. This has always been in the cards. That decision was made long ago, but I think it's important you understand, really understand, Karin, what's about to happen."

"All right, then."

She could still hear herself breathing.

Dream slapped the floor with the cable.

She noticed that the fog had dissipated and the wind was tearing through the dry reeds. A black-throated loon flew over the lake.

There was an unfamiliar spot on the window, sticky and whitish, that she hadn't noticed before. She stared at the spot for a while, until she felt compelled to turn her attention back to the woman.

"Your earnings and expenditures from the past years have been assessed, your travels and the ownership of, among other things, this house. Which is mortgage-free."

She watched how the woman's face moved as she spoke. The pores along the sides of her nose were enlarged, some clogged. Reluctantly, she met her gaze.

"And the taxable liquid assets have been assessed, but you know that. You've also been referred to the Tax Agency, but you have yet to make a payment."

She looked at the woman, at the paper on the table, and felt the room shift. It fell away behind her, the floor opened up, the walls slid apart, she looked at Dream.

"When will it happen?" she asked.

"Well, the requisition is scheduled for next week, so that means, it'll be, ah, in nine days. And at that time we'll also seize a vehicle, meaning your car . . . the one parked outside, correct?"

"I guess."

The large black-and-white bird rose in the sky, its wings outstretched. One of them seemed to be pointing straight up into the heavens. The bulletproof glass didn't let in any noise, but she imagined the bird's cry pulsing over the lake, over everything on the other side of the windowpane.

"Where am I supposed to go?"

She hadn't meant to say that out loud.

As if to underscore the humiliation, the woman didn't respond. Something surged from the void within.

Nausea.

The child started crying and she went over and lifted her up, rocking her and pressing her against her chest, against her pounding heart, and then walked across the floor.

If they were speaking, she couldn't hear them.

She gazed through the window at the lake. She searched for the pair of swans and spotted them in a thicket of reeds, nuzzling each other, their heads tucked into their wings, the snow close to their feathers, which were waxy and not quite white.

She bounced Dream on her hip and walked back to them.

"I thought you might have questions," said the woman. "And if there's anything I can't answer, Göran here can help." She gestured toward the man. He set his coffee cup down and cleared his throat.

She didn't have any, but he jumped in anyway.

"We follow the money," he said. He seemed to think he was introducing her to a new concept.

"I'm sure you know that's how we fight organized crime nowadays. It reduces the incentive for this type of serious crime that creates so many problems. For everybody. The kind no one wants in a modern society."

She nodded and looked at him. An administrator at the Enforcement Authority. Sitting there in his plaid shirt and looking at her as if he fancied himself some sort of hero.

She noticed herself bouncing Dream far too vigorously. Took a breath and stared at the floor, trying to calm down. She studied the grain on the parquet and listened to the man drone on about how a locksmith would pay her a visit when the time came, about the storage of furniture and how certain personal items—food and clothing and dirty laundry—would be handled, if anything like that was left in the house.

"It's best if you clear everything out yourself," he said. "Now. Before the eviction. And do the cleaning. If you don't want to incur any additional costs."

He was speaking faster all of a sudden.

When she leaned toward him, she noticed he had a smell, and that smell was fear. So, she wasn't just anybody after all.

She stood in front of him.

He fell silent.

"Is that it?" she asked, raising her voice over Dream's, who had begun to cry.

The woman nodded.

"Yes, unless you—"

"Then you can show yourselves out."

"Do you have anywhere to go?" the woman asked as she got up to leave.

She didn't reply.

"Social Services will be looped in too, you know."

As she ascended the stairs, she heard the woman say: "You're not alone, Karin. Trust me, there are lots of girls in your situation."

She stopped.

"I doubt that very much," she said. "I don't think you have any idea what you're talking about."

While they were still watching, she went into the bedroom and closed the door. Rage overpowered her—an iron hand clamping her head and squeezing her mind in its vise until only a slim ray of light and reality remained.

She took a deep breath.

Dream quieted down as soon as her head met the bed. The baby was exhausted. She lay next to her; placed a hand on her soft, hot body; and listened. Beyond her own beating heart, she heard the front door slam, a car start and drive off.

THE AIR in the bedroom was stuffy. The bed felt damp. Dried pools of breast milk and urine, patches of drool, and globs of spit-up splotched the champagne-colored satin sheets. On both of the nightstands and on the floor lay empty packets of Tylenol, tubes of Voltaren, and old nursing pads. Dirty towels and crumpled wet wipes were strewn among glasses and bowls crusted with leftovers.

Her arm was wrapped around Dream.

She stared at the ceiling.

The little one woke up, but fell right back asleep; she let go of her, rolled over, and tried to picture John, but it took her a moment.

This was a recent development. She'd first noticed it on New Year's Eve. Dream was sick and had finally drifted off and she wanted to treat herself by fantasizing about him, but his face was hazy.

The space around his jaw seemed to have been erased, as if she couldn't remember its contours or what his stubble looked like.

She opened the drawer on the nightstand and took out the old cell phone. She dialed her voice mail and covered the speaker to block out that loathsome automated female voice. She hated it because it had become a witness. When it was done, John's voice materialized:

"Hey you. Whatcha doin'?"

A rustling sound. Maybe he was scratching under his collar.

"So, I was thinking. How 'bout we go kayaking this weekend? I realized . . . Well. I gotta spend some time outside. Okay. Mwah."

The beep that signaled the end of the voice mail cut into her. Then came another recording, filled only with the sound of breathing, static, and a click. Followed by a beep and then a shorter message:

"Hey, bring my sunglasses, will you? They're in the hall."

She sat in the large bed clutching the phone and crying, letting his voice consume her. With each syllable, a room opened up containing everything he was to her and everything she believed she'd been to him. Their entire life as a couple seemed to be encapsulated in each of his ordinary words, in how he said them and strung them together, how they hung there between him and her.

She buried her face in the bedding, felt her mouth open, and heard herself scream into the fabric and the feather-down. She soaked the sheets around her and tensed her body so much that her legs lifted off the bed. She cried and cried until her cries were as dry as shouts. Enough already, she thought, this must be the last of it. And behind that thought: there was no end.

She sat up.

Blew her nose and lit a cigarette she'd found in the bed; the nicotine reconstituted her. She looked out the window, where the snowy crowns of two pine trees swayed against the murky sky, and hoped that Dream wouldn't wake to find her crying.

That's how it is. At first, you're cautious, bearing the terrible weight of having someone else's life in your hands and of bringing a child into a family like this. And then you relax. It doesn't matter as much anymore. What will be will be. The child is at your mercy. You and the child are one and the same.

Fast asleep, Dream pursed her lips and put her hands by her head.

She closed her eyes and let her thoughts churn.

It was time. She had to get going.

S HE HAD showered and was standing in front of her closets. Freezing, but at least the cold water had perked her up. She scrutinized the countless white specks of dust powdering the mirrored sliding doors, and then reluctantly focused on herself: her tired, sallow face blotchy from crying; wet ropy hair; delicate scratches covering her breasts.

Dream's nails were always a little too long. They were hard to get at with the file and she was afraid of nicking her fingertips with the nail clippers again. At the pediatrician's office, they told her that with a tiny baby, the nails should be torn or bitten off.

She didn't like catching her reflection whenever she passed the closet unit, and would have preferred to keep the doors open but didn't dare. She didn't know how the closets were anchored to the wall and if they'd fall over if Dream tried to crawl into them.

She slid one of the doors aside and peered in.

So much had been sold, but there was plenty left. Neat stacks of shirts folded with tissue paper, belts on hooks, lace panties in drawers, and handbags lined up on shelves.

Footwear stuffed with paper and shoe trees. Rows of garments on hangers made of wood or padded silk.

It was surreal.

As if she'd lost one of her senses.

She opened a drawer and took a pair of gauzy stockings from one of the compartments. She pulled them on and rolled them up her legs. Pale stubble stuck through the nylon. She searched for the tricot dress with a zipper that ran all the way down the front; she slipped it on and pulled a sweater over it. She picked out a pair of black ankle boots and a black rabbit-fur jacket, which she couldn't remember ever wearing, but there was a pack of gum and an almost full packet of cigarettes in one of the pockets, so she must have worn it at least once.

THE PARKING lot was covered with snow, ice, and sand that had been strewn to make it less slippery. The towering white high-rises ahead were like an island in a suburban sea of endless nothing: highways, viaducts, apartment complexes. The snow obscured remnants of mountains and forests that had given way to civilization.

Soon darkness would fall. The sky was heavy with the promise of snow. A heightened gray, the color of the asphalt, patches of which showed through.

The gas tank was almost empty.

She gingerly closed the car door and walked around. Her hair was still damp and a few strands froze to her face. They crunched when she brushed them to the side and tucked her hair into her jacket.

She was on her own and had nothing. Nothing but a child she was obliged to care for. Her face burned with the memory of each warning she'd received.

Those thoughts were hard to face.

Everybody had said it would turn out like this.

Of course, she too had predicted that she'd end up alone. She had thought of it often, in fact. The nightmares she'd had about his body, his beating heart, his face—crushed. He'd take a seat at the kitchen island with his newspaper and turn to her, his face a black-bloody mess.

She'd been terrified of losing him. At times bracing herself, at times forcing it out of her mind. But she hadn't expected to lose everything else along with him.

Dream was asleep in the backseat with her fleece hood pulled over her eyes. She succeeded in stuffing Dream's hands into her mitten cuffs, unfastening the seat belt, and taking out the car seat without waking her up. As she gripped the handle she thought she could feel his hand holding it too: his warm palm, his fingers and fingertips, their touch as real as Dream's had been just now.

He bought the car seat.

It was the only thing he'd had a chance to buy.

She hung it on her forearm even though the baby made it too heavy to carry that way. It would leave a bruise.

After she'd locked the car and put the key in her pocket, she paused. There was no one else around. She clutched her jacket at the collar and started to walk, noticing that she was tensing her upper body in an attempt to fend off the cold or perhaps force it into submission.

Her ankle boots had slim heels and shiny soles. The dark ice on the ground was dusted with snow. She stepped onto the road, telling herself not to slip, and then slipped.

She managed to lift the car seat into the air before she lost her grip on it, fell, and let it land on her body. She shrieked.

And then it was as quiet as before.

Tears welled in her eyes.

She got to her feet and brushed herself off, shaking.

Her cheeks burned. Pain shot out from her tailbone.

Dream was screaming.

She continued along the icy asphalt, trying to rock the baby while taking small steps—avoiding icy patches and puddles, head down, and holding the car seat so the wind was out of Dream's face.

This nothing place.

A few streetlights lined the walkway leading out of the parking lot. A park bench and a low post from what was once a trash can but was now just charred remains. From the stairs, you could see the bus stop and the back of a shopping center; its roof was covered in graffiti and full of trash that teenagers and homeless people had left behind. In the distance, the highway was a river flowing away from her. Other islands of high-rise apartments.

She held on to the cold railing and her bare palm froze to it. When she'd reached the top of the stairs, she moved the car seat farther down her arm and continued along the path.

She noticed herself trembling.

Dream was quietly letting herself be rocked.

She entered the courtyard. Two groups of young men were hanging around outside the buildings; they circled each other like amoebas in the dark. Heated conversation, cell phones glowing, spitting, and throwing punches and kicks. Clouds of breath floated between them. She walked by, eyes fixed to the ground; she was just a mother out with her baby, nothing more, and yet their laughter and banter stopped as she passed.

They mumbled to each other, and then shouted after her.

She didn't look back; she kept going. Trying to step only where there would be friction—a piece of gravel, frozen or packed snow, bare asphalt. During her fall, she'd broken a nail. Watery blood rimmed the break and she pressed her thumb against it.

In the tiled corridor leading to the building's entrance a man in a baggy leather jacket and gabardine trousers was smoking, jumping in place, and kicking a small mound of snow. He nodded in her direction when she went by, but she ignored him. When she walked through the unlocked door, she was surprised he'd gone outside for a cigarette; the stairwell stank of smoke.

Dream had freed her hand from one mitten and was holding on to the edge of the car seat, fast asleep. Huddled together on the stairs next to the elevator were two whispering girls. She said hello and felt them watching her as she got into the elevator. There was only one apartment on the top floor. Alex's penthouse. A nasty dump of a penthouse, but whatever.

The first thing she noticed was that he'd installed a security system and a video intercom at the front door. She set the car seat down on the landing and looked at the sleeping creature, her little mouth fixed in a determined line.

She hadn't been here since it happened.

She couldn't stop staring at the sturdy steel frame around the door. For a moment, she stood perfectly still.

Even the reinforcement on the door was made of polished steel. The mail slot was sealed shut with large bolts, and there was a faint mark where the old doorbell had once been, a hole that had been spackled but not painted over.

She stood up straighter and tensed her lips out of habit. She rang the new bell, assuming her face would instantly appear on a screen somewhere inside. Waited, listened to the locks rolling into place, and when the door opened she couldn't remember if she'd seen the guy before. He was probably one of the young thugs Alex surrounded himself with nowadays, this kid with bad skin and tube socks who was looking at her and Dream, not saying a word.

Maybe he didn't know who she was.

She probably wasn't special anymore.

The air in the apartment was thick with weed. He showed them in and vanished. Therese's voice came from one of the rooms, cracking, raspy.

And then there she was, right in front of her.

How odd. After all the time that had gone by, the many days without phone calls, without seeing each other, she'd almost expected a stranger. But it was just Therese, lounging around. The sweet, familiar scent of her black hair. She remembered exactly how it felt when they were skin to skin.

And yet, here they were. Estranged.

Therese just sat there, didn't even look up.

She'd never really considered how different they were. As she looked at Therese lazing on Alex's leather sofa, watching a television set hung like a painting, she thought about how ironic it was that now, when they weren't quite so different, they were no longer close.

Therese still hadn't looked at her, even though she was standing right there. Eyes riveted to the screen, she didn't seem to want to acknowledge her presence: pies and cakes were being filled and frosted, tasted, glazed with egg whites, and placed in ovens. Without looking over, she greeted her with something that was not quite a wave. "Sorry," she said. "I don't feel like getting up."

Her arms hung limply at her sides; her legs were resting on that dark coffee table Alex had always had. She was barefoot, her slim toes crowned by a French pedicure that looked as soft as her brand-new pink velour tracksuit.

She couldn't stop staring at Therese, but she didn't want her voice to betray her when she replied.

"No worries," she said as she put the car seat on the floor and rocked it gently.

Therese's hoodie was unzipped, revealing the top of her tattoo. She had dark circles under her eyes, but her cheekbones seemed higher and her lips were pouty and glossed. Her skin was pale and flecked with pimples and other blemishes that hadn't been there before, but her face shimmered supernaturally in the dim light of the room. Her nails shone too, and on each hand the letters FUCK were painted in black over a glaring polish.

Empty bottles of Vitaminwater were strewn on the table, along with an ashtray filled with cigarette butts and half-smoked joints. She unfastened Dream's overalls, fingering the smooth fleece and the small snaps, gazing at her soft, peaceful face. She'd been at Dream's side since the day she was born. How would it feel to leave her here?

She slipped off the child's booties and her beanie, so she could keep sleeping without getting too hot.

She took a seat on the sofa.

Finally, Therese looked at her.

Her eyes were dull and dark. The gleam they'd had when they were friends wasn't there anymore. She'd been missing it for a long time, but now she realized she had developed a sense of ownership over it; it was like a lost possession.

"Want anything?" Therese asked, glancing at Dream, who was sleeping with her mouth wide open. "I'm going to have a Vitaminwater. Okay? Can you drink that?"

"Yes."

"Nothing for her?"

"No."

Therese turned around without getting up and shouted into the dark hall: "Hey!"

No answer.

"Dumbass."

She turned again and shouted.

"Stop jerking off, you fucking retard!"

Dream twitched in the car seat and flung out her arms as if she were falling and then fell right back asleep.

Therese sighed.

"I'll get them," she said, and Therese nodded listlessly.

She got up and walked down the hall that led through the rest of the apartment to the kitchen. The walls, covered with ingrain wallpaper, were otherwise bare and marred with dirt and black scuffs. The rooms she passed seemed desolate. In a couple, she glimpsed boxes and cartons piled on top of each other, mattresses on the floor that must have been put there so the guys could crash—boys who arrived at night with their haul and didn't have anywhere better to be afterward. People who might think of this place as a sort of home.

In the hallway was a large safe on a dolly. She stopped for a closer look: the sleek metal handle, the lock and keypad, steel fibers glinting in the fluorescent lights overhead.

The apartment was silent.

She forced herself to move along, trying not to make a sound so no one would notice she'd stopped by the dolly and get it into their heads that she'd been eyeing the safe.

The kid who'd let her in was nowhere to be seen.

On a table in the kitchen were a few cartons of cigarettes and bundles of ten-kronor scratch-off tickets. The Vitamin-water was in the fridge and she took two bottles. Passing the safe on her way back, she felt queasy. She wondered what Alex was going to do with it and if he'd be home soon.

In the living room, the TV show was interrupted by a commercial break and Therese turned to her with an expression that might even have been a smile.

"Time to get those tits out!" she said.

"Ugh, I'm so over them." She sat down and unscrewed the caps off both bottles.

"You shouldn't be."

"I've missed you."

Therese replied by running her tongue over her bleached front teeth and her gums, which were slightly inflamed. Therese glanced in Dream's direction and said:

"I get it. It's been heavy."

That was one way of putting it.

She nodded and downed nearly half the bottle in one syrupy gulp. She steeled herself and asked:

"Do you know if Alex owes John anything?"

"Huh?"

She shouldn't have been so quick to ask. Therese raised her eyebrows and shook her head slowly, as if the question came as such a shock she wanted to be sure she wasn't dreaming.

"*That's* why you're here?"

"Yeah. I was wondering if there was anything with my name on it." Therese shook her head again. "But I also came over because I've been missing you."

Therese coughed and singed the filter of the cigarette she was trying to light. The tattoo draped across her chest like a necklace: *Non, je ne regrette rien*. She looked up at her and exhaled a stream of smoke.

"You've got *money*."

"No, I don't."

It made her uncomfortable to say it out loud.

"What?"

"It's gone. The money's gone and nothing is on its way."

"You don't have a stash somewhere?"

"No. Well, I don't know. There might be some somewhere. Understand?"

She got to her feet and pointed at the balcony door, so Therese put on a pair of bunny slippers, ears dragging on the floor. They went to the balcony.

"What's the matter?"

"I haven't heard anything and no one's talked to me, so I'm wondering what you might know." She was trying to sound cool and collected.

"About what?"

"If there's anything for me . . . that's mine." She looked down at the people milling around in the courtyard. "I'm surprised no one's sent anything my way. You know, after all that stuff about having each other's backs."

Staring at a crumbly crack running across the concrete floor, Therese gave a brief nod. She smirked and a whistling sound escaped from her mouth.

"Oh honey, I'm sorry," she said, and made eye contact. "Were you expecting to sit out there in your big pretty house and wait for someone to drop off a bag of cash?"

"Sure, why not? Everyone's always going on about how we're a family."

Therese looked at her as if she was clueless, as if giving birth had made her lose her mind. Then Therese nodded and asked:

"Why didn't you talk to me?"

"I'm talking to you now."

She nodded again and gazed out over the courtyard ringed by the housing projects built as part of the Million Program.

"Why don't you just sell your house?" she said.

"That was supposed to be the plan, so I didn't make other arrangements. I was supposed to be able to sell it, but I can't." She took out a cigarette from the old packet, lit it, and forced herself to say:

"They're taking the house."

"What?"

"Yeah."

"But it's *your* goddamn house. You're just a regular citizen."

"They made their calculations. They're *following the money*," she said with a derisive twitch.

"So, if your man or dad or son or whoever is on the list, they could, like, take anything they want?"

"Pretty much. If they're on the list."

"I thought that list wasn't real."

"Oh, it's real."

Therese paused.

"Fuck their fucking list! Fuck it all to hell! Goddamnit!" Therese gripped the balcony railing and kicked the metal fencing so hard it sang. Then she stared into the distance, flicked her cigarette, and whistled through her front teeth. "Fuck!" she exclaimed, slapping the railing. "So then there's nothing you can fucking do."

"No. But you never know who's on the list."

"I bet Alex knows . . ."

Darkness had fallen.

"At least he *should* know," Therese said, and stubbed out her cigarette.

They went back inside.

She sat on the sofa. Her tailbone ached.

She hid her expression.

"I don't know how to help you," Therese said, and it almost sounded as though she enjoyed this role reversal. "Alex, he . . . I don't know, it's up to him. You get that, right?"

She nodded and swallowed. Therese met her eyes. She felt like crying.

"But, come on, the fuck you want me to do!" she hissed.

"I don't know. Talk to him, maybe? Tell him I'm being left out in the cold?"

She'd never asked anyone for help before and she had imagined it would take a concerted effort, but as soon as she opened her mouth, something happened. She desperately wanted to tell Therese everything—how lonely she was and how hopeless she felt and how she'd never cut anyone out the way they had done to her.

But she held back.

She'd already been too impatient once.

"All that talk about having each other's backs. It was just *talk*, wasn't it?" she said.

She buried her head in her hands and waited for Therese to put a hand on her shoulder. When she didn't and nothing else was said, she felt the weight of the air around her. Her heart pounded. So she was alive after all.

When she looked up, Therese seemed to be on a high ledge, staring down at her, taking pleasure in seeing her at the bottom of the ravine.

And she heard herself make another plea:

"I thought you might know if anyone owed John anything."

"Gawd, Karin. I don't know! Why would *I* have any intel? Alex doesn't fucking talk to me!"

"I just thought that we . . . *know* a lot. Even if we're not supposed to. Right?"

She wasn't sure how eager Therese was to rekindle their friendship, maybe she didn't even want to, so she didn't mention how much their relationship had changed. She didn't have to; it was right there between them. To distract herself, she took Dream out of the car seat and held her close to rouse her with the scent of milk. She pushed up her sweater, unzipped her dress, and took out one of her breasts. Dream's lips searched and suctioned themselves to her nipple.

Therese lit another cigarette.

Other than the television, the only sound that could be heard was Dream feeding. One little hand was stuffed behind her back and the other was gripping her sweater. Every now and then Dream took a break and let go of the sweater, waving her hand and scratching her breast with her small, dirt-rimmed nails.

"I get that you're having a hard time," Therese said, in a tone that suggested she was speaking about a natural state of affairs, a situation that no one was accountable for and that, above all, she played no part in.

Therese belonged to Alex now, her life revolved around him and he determined the conditions of their shared existence.

Dream burped and seemed to be smiling. Milk dribbled from her mouth, as though it were impossible to drink another drop. When she held her upright, her body gurgled. Shuddered. And then there was a bubbling sound. Her diaper had a sour smell.

Without thinking, she handed Dream to Therese, who wrinkled her nose and held her away from her body. Dream laughed and drooled. She took out diapers and wet wipes and the mat, unfolded the diaper bag so it became a bed. She put it on the sofa, placed Dream on top, and unsnapped the snaps on her onesie.

"Why doesn't it have a zipper?" Therese asked.

"I know, right?"

She began undoing the diaper.

"I guess they think we don't have anything better to do than deal with these snaps."

Therese looked pained and fascinated when she saw the yellow mess in the diaper.

"What the hell is she eating?"

She smiled.

Dream clucked when she lifted up her legs so she could wipe her properly, then she folded the wet wipe with one hand and placed it on the diaper. She noticed that Therese couldn't help looking at the baby's soft body and her little genitals, a perfect shell of white skin that she still didn't have a word for.

When she was done, she rolled up the diaper into a package and sealed it with the strip of tape. Then she dressed Dream in her onesie, relieved that it hadn't been soiled at the back, and propped her up on the sofa with a cushion. She left clean diapers and wet wipes on the table, and from her handbag she took a bottle and a carton of formula.

"Could you watch her for me?" she asked.

Silence.

"Me?" Therese asked.

"Yes."

"No way!"

"Come on. Of course you can. It'll only be for a little while. Plus, there's nobody else who can take her."

Therese looked at her skeptically.

"Please?"

She sat Dream on Therese's lap and tore open the carton with her teeth and poured it into the bottle.

"There's no one else."

"Where are you going?"

"I have a meeting."

"Is it a guy?"

"No!"

It was clear that Therese wasn't going to give in unless she knew exactly what was happening. She sighed and threw open her arms. "I'm meeting Christer, okay!"

"I see."

Therese nodded suspiciously.

She put Dream's pacifier on the table and pointed at the charger cable.

"She can play with that," she said.

The gang was still in the courtyard. A pack of hyenas in black jackets, craning their necks, staring into the darkness. They whistled as she walked by.

She knew what Therese was thinking: Shit happens and it can happen to anyone. And she knew Therese was right. Shit happens to everyone. But she had yet to accept that "everyone" included her.

S HE WAS on time. Being out alone, without the stroller, was surreal. It was as if something had been dislodged from her body. Riding the escalator up from the subway, she remembered how it used to feel. Anticipation flickered inside her as soon as she began to rise toward the city. Nothing like what she was feeling now.

There was barely any snow on these streets. They charted a dark course between ornate stone buildings, slipping under taxi wheels and reflections of light, people charging into the night, window displays demanding attention. Outside the subway's entrance, she slowed as she passed the homeless people lying near the hot vent, maneuvered around them, and made her way to the crosswalk. On the other side of the street was a man glowing in the dark, his face shadowy and gaunt. He was pushing a wheeled neon-green trash can that matched his clothing.

She crossed and he stayed put, tracking her with a steady, penetrating stare as she passed by him.

Through the restaurant window, she caught sight of Christer seated at a table and paused at the door to make sure the five-hundred-kronor bill was still in her pocket. Each time they met he apologized for it not being under happier circumstances and he picked up the tab, but she didn't want to take any chances.

She backed out of his field of vision and smoked a cigarette, hoping he wouldn't decide to step out for one too. She needed time to collect herself and stood just beyond the outdoor patio, where empty tables and chairs jostled for space under a narrow awning and heat lamps. This might be the place where everything that had gone wrong would be made right. When she emerged from the restaurant, everything might be different.

She took a deep breath. Tossed her cigarette into the street.

On her way in, she caught her reflection in the glass pane of the door a man was holding open for her.

Inside, it was warm. The faux French brasserie smelled of dank coats and fried meat. Christer had left the banquette to her. She'd be facing the room. Everyone would see her, and then look at him.

He stood to greet her at the table, kissed both cheeks, took her hand in his, looked at her, and smiled.

"Karin!"

Her tailbone twinged when she sat down across from him. A waitress filled her water glass, he placed their order, and she said "yes" and nodded at everything he said, though she wasn't really catching what he was saying.

She spread her napkin over her lap.

The marble tabletop.

The bread basket.

One breath at a time.

"You look stunning, really you do," he said.

She tried to smile.

He spoke quickly, piling word upon word. Asking her how she was doing, about Dream, about her plans, if she was still considering going to college, what her thoughts were on what had happened, now, in the aftermath.

"It feels like yesterday," she said.

"Right, right," he said.

"But Dream won't let me forget that it isn't."

"Tell me about it. They grow up so fast. It's such a cliché, but, well . . . You'll never get these moments back."

He looked at her and a silence descended.

He was slightly sunburned.

"I'm truly sorry, Karin," he said. "You know I am."

She nodded.

Outside, it had begun to snow.

"And I know everyone is saying this, because that's the way it is, but I sincerely hope you can find a way to enjoy this time with her."

She nodded and her breasts ached.

"It's hard for everyone," he continued. "I tried to focus on quality time with mine. But that's not right, now is it?"

She shook her head.

He told her about his vacation.

She struggled to pay attention, shifting on the banquette, trying to seem engaged while dark flowers of pain bloomed at the base of her spine. The spot felt sticky too, as if it were skinned.

As he was holding forth, she excused herself.

In the restroom she tore off a sheet of toilet paper, stood on her tiptoes in front of the mirror, lifted her dress, and pulled down her stockings and panties. A purplish blush had spread across one of her cheeks. When she looked closer she saw a pattern of small abrasions where the blood had pushed through and formed pinhead-like droplets. She tried to wipe them away, but it was too painful. She held a compress of wet paper towels to her skin.

When she came out of the restroom, a blond woman nodded at her in recognition and someone at another table stood to greet her. She tried to smile, but couldn't remember who they were.

An older man had stopped by their table, laughing loudly and shrilly at something Christer was saying, but when she reached them, he walked away without saying hello. A minor relief. She sat down delicately, but the pain asserted itself and she winced. Swallowed.

A plate was placed in front of her.

Her knife sank right through the fibers of the flesh, red juice pooling on the white plate.

She ate quickly. When the meal was over, Christer leaned in.

"On the phone, it sounded as if there was something you wanted to discuss," he said.

She put down her glass.

He was about to start talking again. She jumped in.

"I was wondering, is it possible he was working with some-one I might not've known about?" she asked. "Who might've borrowed . . . or embezzled . . . some money."

He fidgeted in his seat and wiped his mouth with his napkin.

"I see," he said.

He let go of the napkin, chuckled, and squeezed the horn-handled knife, pointing the curved blade in her direction.

"So, you think I'm some sort of David Kleinfeld."

"Excuse me?"

He rested the knife on his plate and settled into his chair.

"A lawyer who's worse than his client! Haven't you seen that movie? What's it called . . . I can't remember. Typical."

He shrugged and leaned over the table and held her gaze. When he laughed, she caught a glimpse of his tongue.

"Are you being serious?"

"Yes."

"Do you need money?"

She nodded.

"The Tax Agency is taking the house. I'm losing it."

His expression changed. Pity. He sighed and took a deep breath.

"So the Enforcement Authority is getting the house?"

"Yes."

"And they've served you with a notice of levy?"

"Yes."

"I see. Well, they're just doing their job."

She took the paper out of her pocket and handed it to him. He unfolded it, skimmed it. He folded it up and pushed it to her side of the table as if he didn't want it anywhere near him. She quickly put it back in her pocket.

"What a shame," he said. "But there's not much you can do."

She wasn't used to him taking this tone with her. He sounded submissive, as if he considered himself—and by default, her—outmaneuvered.

"Unfortunately, the leeway one has in these situations is minimal."

She replayed this sentence word for word in her head. Aside from the persistent pain, her body seemed to have lost all feeling.

"It's how they're playing it now," he said with a shrug and a wry smile. "You have to admit, it's effective."

She sighed.

He looked down, as if in regret, and glanced up at her.

Neither one of them said anything.

He asked if she wanted coffee and she nodded.

"Now, I haven't been out to visit you both . . . you . . . for a while," he said. "But from what I recall the house is quite something. And the location! Don't get me wrong when I say it was remarkable that someone like John could set himself up like that. And he did it all for you, didn't he?"

"Yes," she said. "I think so."

"We're talking, what . . . twelve, fifteen mil?"

"A real estate agent came by and had a look, but I can't remember."

"Okay. Well, they have to do that, of course, to get a proper appraisal. They can't run around like complete amateurs!"

His gaze was probing.

"I'm guessing," he said, "there'd been a few good years."

She didn't reply, and made a point of keeping her eyes on the marble tabletop.

"Did you really plan on staying there?"

"I'd always thought I could sell the house . . . Whatever happened I thought I'd be able to sell it, so I wasn't really worried . . . about anything."

She was trying not to sound like an idiot.

He was giving her his full attention.

"But it didn't work out that way."

"No, it didn't."

He nodded.

"With this kind of thing, legal certainty might seem questionable," he said. "It hinges on identifying persons of interest and putting them on that list. The GOB list. After that you have to meet a number of criteria regarding insider contacts and violent capital. Then, with these individuals specifically, they decide it's okay to break the usual code of silence, and using intelligence collected by various authorities, they go for the jugular."

He gulped his wine and wiped his mouth. "This kind of thing never used to happen. Staying on top of the suspects, harassment, every means of harassment. Just keeping the pressure on. Parking tickets, Social Security requests, demands for outstanding taxes. You name it. These so-called 'administrative measures.' " He interrupted himself and looked at her.

"Oh, I'm sorry," he said. "I don't need to explain this to you."

"No, you really don't."

And yet he went on: "It's all to get at the alleged key players. And what really hurts . . ." He paused to wave at a blond as she passed their table. "Is when they go after the relatives. Which they always do, if there are any."

She nodded, but couldn't bring herself to comment.

"Will the house cover it?" he asked.

"They're taking my car too."

"Sure, I get that. They've made their calculations. But mind you, they can't take small items. I imagine you have plenty that might be worth a pretty penny. They can't waste their time selling those things, it's not cost-effective."

She tried to stay focused.

"I thought we might be able to appeal," she said.

"I'll absolutely look into it," he said. "I promise I will. But you should probably accept that it won't help. The chances are slim at best."

He tilted forward.

"Honestly, I didn't think it would come to this in your case, but maybe I was being naive. Nowadays they're really doing everything they can to nail people when there's no other recourse for action, or when an organization is as comprehensive as John's and they want to remove the incentives. And let's not forget, it's also a question of making an example of someone. This is, above all, most likely."

"But what do you think," she began. She lowered her voice. "Is it possible part of a, um, profit has been distributed to certain . . . associates . . . and I might be entitled to it?"

He didn't seem to understand.

"I'm wondering if there's anything out there for me to collect."

"You're looking for other resources?"

She nodded.

He shifted in his chair and crossed his legs. He propped his elbows on the table and pressed his fingertips together.

"I know that's what you want, Karin. And I understand how you must be feeling in this situation. You think there must be something you can do. But is this . . . what I'm imagining you're thinking right about now . . . really a prudent course of action? See what I'm getting at?"

She looked him in the eye.

"In all these years, you've never gotten involved, not even once. Right, Karin?"

She shook her head.

"And I'd say that was a smart move."

"Yes, maybe. You never know."

"Sure, sure, but let's assume it was. I haven't gotten involved either. I don't know what impression you have of me, but I'm really just a simple lawyer. I've never been initiated into any of their activities. I've come into contact only with matters that directly relate to the law and jurisprudence."

He wiped his mouth with his napkin; for a moment it covered most of his face.

"Wouldn't you say that you and I, we're cut from the same cloth?"

She tried to nod. Suddenly, she felt exhausted.

"I'm not sure how it would serve you to get involved," he continued. "We all have sides to ourselves that we choose to keep hidden. Going down that road could come with its surprises . . . even if you think you know a number of those fellows."

"Sure."

"I'm guessing that road leads to nowhere. You're a smart cookie, Karin."

She didn't know what to say.

She wasn't seeing him clearly; the air in front of his face seemed to be trembling. But she understood what he was saying. For the first time since they'd known each other, he couldn't tell her everything was going to be okay.

She'd had enough. She wanted to get up from the table, walk right out the door, and disappear into the night.

A waitress brought coffee, which she hadn't noticed him order. And a small glass that held something sharp, numbing, but not enough.

She was having difficulty breathing.

The gentle hum, heat from the candles everywhere, the kitchen smells, the waitstaff's happy masks, and the conversation buzzing around the tables—it all seemed to be stealing the oxygen. Almost unbearably intrusive, insisting on a certain kind of happiness that she didn't want to be reminded of; it seemed even further out of reach now than it had only hours ago.

She was relieved when he suggested they get the bill. He took out his card and placed it on the silver tray before the waitress had a chance to set it on the table. Once again, he asked if she hadn't considered moving out, whatever the case, and then he asked about her family. Couldn't they help?

Her reply was brief, because every word weighed down her tongue.

They took their things from the cloakroom, which was stuffed with furs and overcoats. He helped her with her jacket and something in the gesture of hanging it over her shoulders made her feel very alone. She was more alone now than when she'd walked into the restaurant.

She wanted to leave right away, but once they were outside, he offered her a cigarette. He held out the packet and said he was happy there were still smokers in the world, laughing as though this might cheer her up.

"Let's make one more stop, shall we?" he said. "A little distraction might be nice."

She didn't know how she'd manage another word. She gathered what little strength she had left and said:

"No. I have to pick up Dream."

"Can't it wait?"

"No, it can't."

She hugged him quickly and kissed him on the cheek. Waved and smiled. Knew which way he'd be going and went in the other direction. Without the stroller, she thought the wind might lift her off the ground and blow her away like a crumpled receipt.

She crossed a heated plaza framed by a wavy crust of black ice. The first drunks of the evening were staggering around. People were lined up outside of crowded bars and she remembered standing in those places, encircled by gazes. She took it all in, but felt like a foreigner, someone who shouldn't spend too much time looking because they didn't belong.

WHEN SHE got back to Alex's apartment it was shortly after midnight. Dream was in Therese's lap and didn't seem to notice her arrival, but Therese turned around right away. And smiled.

"God, she looks so much like him."

"I know."

She kept her eyes on the TV because she couldn't bear the sight of Therese while those words were resonating.

Another episode of the same baking show. Dream's little socks with the grippy rubber stars on the soles were on the table, along with the bottle decorated with a laughing bear holding a balloon.

When she sat down next to them on the sofa, it hurt, and the milk began to seep out. Her bra would be stained white.

"So, what did he say?" Therese asked.

"Nothing. Basically, it's fucked."

"Huh. Screw that guy."

"Right. Anyway, thanks for helping me out."

"What are you going to do now?"

"I have no idea."

She adjusted her clothing, put Dream to her breast. Swollen, rock hard. Dream opened her mouth and tried to latch on, but she couldn't get a grip; her pointy tongue darted helplessly at her nipple, her areola, and the straining skin. Thin streams of milk sprayed Dream's face and eyes.

"I still think there's something you could do to help." A sweat broke out on her forehead.

Therese looked confused.

Dream screamed.

A sound came from somewhere inside the apartment.

She got a better grip on Dream, stood up, and bounced her gently.

The little mouth latched on. She fed.

She sat, exhaled, and rested her head against the sofa. Milk dribbled from the other breast and she made no attempt to stop it. Her dress was already wet.

Therese had lain down on the far end of the sofa. She didn't think Therese was asleep, but she didn't have the energy to keep a conversation going, and anyway, what would she say? She still didn't have a plan. She needed to come up with one, but she couldn't think straight. She tried to account for every hurdle, but there were too many. Following any thought through to the end was tough; it seemed to demand an enormous physical effort and she wasn't strong enough. Sentences dissolved in her mind and by the time she'd caught the next train of thought, the previous one was gone.

And then she heard the front door open.

Someone entering the apartment.

She stayed put with Dream in her arms, closed her eyes, and waited for whoever it was to come into the room.

Therese quickly rolled over.

Several people came in. Men.

She sensed them watching her from the doorway and pretended to be asleep. Sleep would have been nice. She heard Alex ordering the others around, heard them going deeper into the apartment.

Dream gurgled.

She pretended to wake up and opened her eyes. He was leaning against the door, staring at her.

She sat up.

"Whoops," he said.

The look he was giving her made her unlatch Dream from her breast, pull her sweater down over her dress, and get up. At first she'd sensed something like tenderness in his eyes, but it had disappeared in a flash—if it had been there at all.

"So, you want her to take care of your kid now, huh?" he said, pointing at Therese.

Therese was curled up, back turned, motionless on the sofa. She didn't look as if she was sleeping.

"I had to go to a meeting."

"What exactly do you think any of us here owes you?"

"I came over because I need help," she said.

"And?"

"They're taking the house. I'll be left with nothing."

She didn't know what was happening. Or if it had been the right thing to say, but it wouldn't matter what she said, because apparently Therese couldn't keep her mouth shut. She held Dream tighter and put her face close to the child's head.

It only seemed to make him angrier. As though he wanted to hit them.

"Sure, sure," he said, nodding several times. "You have a family, right? A rich dad who'll hook you up with a place in the fucking city if you ask nicely? Get them to help."

"I can't."

Voices came from within the apartment; someone was calling Alex, but he kept staring at her and Dream.

"Okay," he said again. "Time to go."

She stayed put.

"Get out!"

He cracked her on the shoulder. A small movement, but enough to make her lose her balance, and she nearly fell over with Dream.

Therese didn't move.

She pulled on the rest of her clothes and Dream's. She was sure Therese was awake and said her name out loud.

Nothing.

Therese didn't turn around.

"She's not your friend anymore," Alex said. "And you got no business hanging around here."

She clutched Dream.

His face hardened, his nostrils flared.

Then he took a step toward her. He jutted his chin, tilted his head back, widened his eyes, and glared at her. A risible look, but she knew he wasn't playing.

It seemed that he was going to head-butt her.

Each time he moved, she flinched in spite of herself.

"So what, you're gonna hit me now?" she said.

She could hear how her smirk was coloring her words.

She couldn't take it back.

The blow she'd been anticipating came in the form of a slap. Precise and burning.

A pain, sharp at first, that sent a ringing through her head. She teared up, but at least she hadn't screamed. Tightening her grip on Dream and protecting her head, she readied herself for more.

But instead of hitting her again, he unlocked the door, grabbed her car seat, and tossed it into the stairwell, where it landed with a clatter. He dragged her out by the arm. She shielded Dream's head and body, and heard herself moan when he shoved her to the ground.

He shut and locked the door.

Silence.

Frightened, Dream stared ahead.

Tears streaming down her cheeks, she hugged Dream tightly and kissed her face. She pulled herself to her knees, crouched, and righted the car seat. The rim had cracked at the front, but she could tape it when they got home, if she could just find that damn tape.

Her hands were shaking.

She got into the elevator, put the car seat on the floor, and buckled in Dream, who was gazing up at her with silent surprise.

ICE NEEDLES pierced the air that night, sailing through the darkness, battering the windshield by the thousands. The car crawled along the highway and the wipers moved as one. She hadn't gotten around to putting the winter tires on. She knew where they were—stacked under a tarp in a corner of the garage—but there was no one she could ask for help. And anyway, winter would be over soon enough.

Sitting hurt, and she was shaking, more out of anger than anything else. Gripping the wheel as she drove, she couldn't stop thinking about Therese. That stupid pink velour outfit of hers, how she turned away from her. She was annoyed by how disappointed she was in her friend.

She had all the information she needed. Right or wrong didn't matter. She was powerless, and the powerless can't call in what they are owed.

That wasn't news.

She should have known it wasn't worth trying.

The black ice on the road twinkled in the headlights, and the oncoming traffic, all shining beams and wide bright lines, sliced through the dark. Cars kept overtaking her. Each time someone leaned on their horn, she flinched, even though she knew full well that she was driving too slowly.

Dream was crying in the backseat.

She should have sat her up front, next to her.

She exited the highway, pulled onto the shoulder, ran to the other side of the car, unfastened the car seat, and moved it. Then she drove, keeping one hand on Dream. Her pacifier kept falling out of her mouth as she screamed, and each time, she popped it back in. Eventually, the pacifier dropped to the floor, and when she tried to catch hold of it by wedging her hand between the gear shift and the seat, she only managed to flick it farther out of reach.

She tried to keep her eyes on the road and to tune out Dream's snuffles and howls. It was hot in the car. Dream's cries waned and her breathing evened out. At the next exit, she was asleep.

As soon as she was inside and sure the front door was securely locked, she kicked off her wet, muddy ankle boots in the hall, walked into the kitchen, set Dream down on the floor in her car seat, and put the five-hundred-kronor bill back in the drawer. There were only two left. And two one-hundred-kronors. Nothing.

She took out the gun and examined it.

Her fingers were frozen stiff. It was heavy and cold, but she held it in front of her, aiming at the window, her own reflection, the darkness outside.

She set the weapon on the kitchen island, went upstairs, and put the child on the bed. Trying not to wake her, she unfastened her overalls and took off her beanie. Then she went into the closet and took the key for the weapons safe from the hook behind his supply of new, unworn running shoes, stacked in their boxes. She stuck the key in the safe's lock and typed in the code.

The door glided open, heavy against her hand. Inside it, weapons were lined up or hanging in rows, black and tan, silver and shining. Pistols, machine guns, AKs, rifles. A hunting permit with a photo and a few other permits were in the compartment on the inside of the door.

There was only one gun she knew how to handle with ease: the CZ down in the kitchen. The one he'd taught her to use at the club where he practiced. He had shown her the safe the day they'd moved into the house, and what had at first been unsettling soon brought comfort. She was neither ashamed nor afraid of it and considered this shift to be the ultimate proof that she'd become a different person. She had liberated herself from everything that had been imposed on her in the regular world and had chosen a new life.

Dream grumbled in her sleep. She went back into the bedroom, bent over her, and put her hand on her forehead—hot—and saw that she was still asleep even though the child's eyes were half-open and once again filled with tears.

She put on a thick hoodie that no longer smelled of him and went downstairs and dug out one of the old cigarettes she'd found. Her body felt fragile and fatigued. Because she couldn't sit comfortably on the stool, she leaned against the kitchen island, smoking and enjoying the silence.

She stayed there, unsure of what else to do with herself. Smoked another cigarette, thinking about how people who choose to fall in love have no one to blame but themselves. If it's even a choice at all. Could she have done more to prevent it? There must have been something she could have done. There was always a choice—the instant you decided to give in, reservations be damned—and she tried to pinpoint the moment it happened.

Actually, the moment had been inconsequential. There had just been something in the way he'd looked at her—how his gaze reassured her that it was going to be them against the world, and yes, she did in fact want that kind of solidarity.

When she'd stood there for so long she no longer minded if Dream woke up, she went upstairs and undressed her. Getting into bed hurt. Lying down, even the tiniest movement, made her ache.

S HE WOKE around four to wailing and crying. Dream's body was tense, her face red and wet, as if she'd been crying for a long time. She sat up, took the child in her arms, and tried rocking her, but the pain in her tailbone was unbearable.

She got out of bed.

Walking hurt less.

Cradling Dream, she went downstairs and turned on the overhead lights. She wandered around with her, round and round between the sofas and the tables and the kitchen island and past the terrace doors.

Dream was hot and her face was slick with saliva and tears. Each scream rang in her ears and exhaustion was like a pillar of salt inside her.

Outside was pitch dark.

After a while she realized it must be the tooth. She put one hand on Dream's back until she couldn't anymore, listening to the screams become resigned, choking sobs. Slowly, the little body relaxed and then she began singing a lullaby. Again and again as she patted the child, heavy in her arms, she hummed the same brief melody, a tune that reminded her of something her own mother had sung. Perhaps when she had been this age. Did the memory of this melody and her mother's song, the closeness and the heat, mean that she was remembering this time in her own life?

Dream had calmed down a bit. With her tiny hand resting on her mother's forearm, the child gasped for air, snuffling with each inhale. Dream was giving her a reproachful look, because who else could be the cause of her unhappiness? But at least she had finished crying.

She stood still and looked outside, but saw only reflections in the glass and the snow piled against the window, its glinting, pitted surface bathed in blue light. She couldn't see the lake or the forest on the far shore—only the bruised winter night and her own shape. The baby's body pressed to hers, a little arm flopped to one side. Her hair grazing the child.

She was a mother; the reflection confirmed it. And yet she didn't seem to exist—standing alone and illuminated in the middle of the large room, like an aquarium in the dark.

WHEN SHE woke, all was still. Dense, tranquil silence inside a house enveloped by winter. Her first thought: she'd rolled on top of Dream in her sleep and suffocated her.

She turned over and saw the child sleeping next to her on the sofa. The thin skin at the dip of her throat trembling with each inhalation. Her soft arms were stretched overhead and a streak of dried milk ran from her mouth across her cheek.

Her rib cage was plump and proud.

The doorbell rang.

The doorbell had woken her.

She leapt up.

Her body was freezing cold and sticky with milk, her neck felt stiff, and on one side of her bottom, the large bruise was spreading. Her breasts were uneven again. She pulled the robe on, knotted the belt, walked to the door, and opened it.

The cold battered her.

His jacket was zipped up.

It was snowing.

It must have been the afternoon.

Snowflakes blew into her face, into her eyes.

He offered her a pizza box.

She accepted it and let him in. The aroma filled the hall.

"I tried to call you," he said.

She backed up, box in hand.

He stepped inside and shut the door.

As far as she knew, he'd never called her.

"You have my number?"

She couldn't remember giving it to him.

"Sure do," he said. "You enter it when you place your order."

She couldn't remember his name, or if he'd ever told her what it was. It was hard to get a handle on their encounters. When she thought about them, they glided away like ice sheets on the lake and disappeared into darkness. She didn't know how many times they'd met, what they'd said to each other, or how it all began.

"I think your cell is off."

She looked at his shoulders as he took off his jacket. Letting her hand detour along his rib cage before hugging him with one arm, the hot pizza box in her other hand.

"Is she asleep?" he asked.

"Yes."

She looked at his shoulders again.

He covered his mouth.

"Oh no! I shouldn't have rung the bell! Sorry."

He followed her into the kitchen. She placed the box on the island, opened the lid, and picked off two white asparagus spears, then tore off a slice of pizza and stuffed it into her mouth.

She sensed him studying her face.

"What happened here?" he asked, touching her cheek.

She left him hanging.

She tore off another piece, gooey and still hot, barely chewing it before swallowing. Shut the lid, licked her mouth clean, and swallowed once more before she draped her arms around his neck and rested her head against his chest.

It always started this way, with these movements. Like a machine warming up.

She led him upstairs, but as usual she wouldn't kiss him and didn't want to have him in her bed or even the bedroom. So they stayed in the hall, against the easy chair—a present from John—in front of her bookshelf.

He'd always referred to it as "your reading chair."

As he pushed into her—nude and bent over the armrest, the fabric chafing her stomach—the chair became something else.

A tree. Her raw, pale body hanging from its branches.

His hands were soft.

A second after she came, he pulled out and ejaculated in his hand. Then he walked through the bedroom into John's bathroom and rinsed his hand in the sink.

She didn't want him in there, but she wouldn't have wanted his cum all over her either.

They stood by the chair, him hugging her from behind, until they heard Dream whimpering downstairs. She retrieved her robe from the floor, put it on, and went to her. He got dressed and treaded lightly after.

"See ya," she said, turning her back to him as she picked up Dream.

She went to the window and stared out over the partly frozen lake, until she heard him say another goodbye.

The front door slammed.

The moped started up.

She found a half-smoked cigarette in the kitchen and lit it.

When she put her down on the sofa, Dream drifted off to sleep.

She went upstairs and into the bedroom. She didn't shower, put on yesterday's clothes, and climbed into bed. Straining to reach the nightstand, she managed to open the drawer and take out the cell phone. She dialed her voice mail and listened— John's breathing, the saliva in his mouth, the movement of his tongue—trying to make herself believe that it was his tongue she'd just felt on her body.

Outside the window, the pines swayed and puffy snow-flakes sailed through the air and settled on the windowsill.

She rested a hand on her belly and imagined her anxiety to be a block of ice, as she'd been taught, and every breath was hot water washing over it. She imagined all that was frozen at her core slowly thawing. Hot water dissolving the ice crystals, making them disappear.

THE SOUND of Dream screaming woke her—strange, muffled screams coming from below. She leapt out of bed, ran down the stairs, and found her inside one of the large kitchen drawers, legs in the air, head among the pots and pans. She shouldn't be able to do that, she shouldn't even have the chance to fall in. She must have crawled to the kitchen, opened the drawer, pulled herself up for a look, and tumbled in.

She got her out, held her close, and comforted her, blood rushing to her head. She felt compelled to scold her. Raised one finger and waggled it.

"No! That's off-limits!"

Her voice sounded strange, shrill.

Dream was red-faced and howling.

She clutched her to her chest.

"There, there," she said, rocking her, kissing her on the head, pressing their cheeks together, hugging her harder, stroking her back, which trembled with each wet snuffle.

She needed to talk to Therese again.

When she picked up her cell phone, she finally understood what he'd been trying to tell her. She couldn't place a call; it disconnected the second she finished dialing. Her service had been shut off.

She fought back tears. She wanted to fling the piece of shit to the floor, but instead, she clung to Dream and started pacing: rocking her in her arms even though she no longer needed soothing.

THE DRIVEWAY was snowed in; the rhododendron bushes and the car parked next to them were blanketed in white. Clearing off the car wouldn't be easy, and driving didn't make sense. What gas was left in the tank might need to be put to better use.

With one of the stale cigarettes dangling from her lips, she propped Dream on her hip and opened the trunk, trying to take the folding stroller out with just one hand.

But she couldn't.

She set Dream down on the snow in her snowsuit and hoped she wouldn't fall over. Just as Dream began to cry, she yanked the damn thing out, pulled the handle, found the release mechanism with her foot, and pressed down. She picked up the child, dusted off the snow, and tucked her in the bunting bag in the stroller. Then she fitted the rain cover around the canopy and, from her handbag, took out a teething toy shaped like a giraffe, handed it to Dream, and started walking.

The small wheels left deep grooves along the edge of the road. They grew stiffer and stiffer with each step until they finally locked. She gave them a kick to dislodge the packed snow, but after only a few yards they were stuck again and so she shoved the stroller along.

The effort made her hot. Snowflakes landed on her face and melted. They floated into her hair, onto her jacket, and dusted the rain cover. She soldiered on, hoping not to run into a neighbor. Around here, people didn't walk, not even when the weather was better. There was no sidewalk, and anyone she knew who came driving along would have no problem pretending not to see her and the stroller.

But no cars, no people were passing by.

A lone crab apple tree stood in the distance.

She walked to the end of the road, past the roundabout, into the park, and down the path lined with katsura trees; their crowns were like brooms sweeping the sky. Tracks crisscrossed between the trees where other mothers had been with their strollers, and beyond them: nature. Soft white vistas, rich earth, and freedom.

Her hands were turning red. She wasn't wearing a hat, a scarf, or gloves. The skin on her knuckles was rough and dry, threatening to crack. Her eyes watered in the cold and clear snot trickled from her nose. Each time she sniffed it back in, the inside of her nostrils froze.

Beyond the park, the landscape was as barren and blanched as she felt inside. In the western sky hung a white wax-paper moon. Only the bus stop and a new luxury housing development broke the even lines beneath it. Above the field and road, the sky was clear. She saw a couple of cars driving in the distance. A truck covered with a dirty tarp.

Though there was a sidewalk here, the snow made it impassable, so she kept to the side of the road, following a snowbank, a long, lumpy mound that seemed to be made of individual snowballs, covered by fresh snow so white and pure it made her think back to a time before there were roads here. Before there were people.

The second she heard a car approaching, she stopped and watched it drive past. Cars were few and far between, but when one appeared, it screamed by at an incredible speed.

She stopped and leaned over the stroller to check on Dream, who was awake and rosy-cheeked, staring at a care label sewn into one of the canopy's seams. She tried to get her blood flowing with a few halfhearted jumps before setting off again, faster now.

WHEN THEY reached the station, the platform was deserted. No one else was waiting for the train. White flames seemed to be lapping at the frosted asphalt and rows of glimmering icicles hung from the station's eaves. Using one of the old iron posts in the middle of the platform, she knocked the snow off her shoes.

She was going to travel twelve stops, change, and then go another ten.

The train arrived like a shot from the white. She climbed aboard, parked the stroller right inside the doors, stepped on the brake, and sat on the aisle, turned so that she could just about reach the stroller's handle. There was no other way to sit. She had to be vigilant. Someone might come out of nowhere and snatch the stroller and the child.

Dream was still awake. As soon as she freed her arms from the bunting bag, Dream started playing with her hands, grabbing her fingers, spreading them out and looking at them, seemingly amazed that they belonged to her and she controlled them.

As usual, the train was practically empty. Sitting nearby were three women who looked like housekeepers. They carried name-brand handbags and wore name-brand jackets—the quilted walking kind, not thick enough for these temperatures—which she assumed were hand-me-downs from their employers. Pilled sweatpants and snow joggers. She couldn't stop staring at them. Their Spanish was peppered with Swedish words—subway, day care, charger—and they seemed to be making an effort to keep their voices down.

The seats were hard and each time the train lurched around a bend, her bottom throbbed. Through the window, she watched black treetops and white sky flying past. The sky, neither light nor dark, was like spilled milk, and the farther south they traveled, with every station they passed and the closer to the city they came, the more the women seemed to relax. Private schools and conference facilities were being advertised above their heads.

She rang his doorbell. It was crazy to return to a place where people didn't think twice about beating her up and wanted nothing more than to watch her fall. But there she was, crawling back to them. Perhaps it was a sign they were a sort of family after all.

Clearly, she thought they belonged together.

They pushed her away, and she asked for more.

Dream had slept through the last stretch of the journey, but now she was awake, blinking at the strip lighting, perhaps in recognition.

She knocked and rang the bell again.

Alex didn't want her there. He didn't want to be reminded of her existence or of right and wrong and that he should do the right thing. She wished Therese would remember that the two of them had been friends from the start. They had known each other first, and their friendship was the catalyst for all of this. Their bond should have been stronger; Therese shouldn't have let someone like Alex come between them. But she didn't know what to say to win her back.

She sat on the hard floor and pulled the stroller toward her. She picked up Dream, stretched out her legs, and put the child on her lap. Looking into her eyes, she jiggled her tiny hands in the air, so she looked like a rapper gesturing in a music video. Dream giggled.

So children *are* a kind of asset, she thought. Bringing her joy, when there was nothing to feel joyful about.

She waited.

When Therese stepped out of the elevator, she made a bee-line for the door and unlocked the locks, one after the other. When she caught sight of them on the floor, she looked weary. Her voice was spent when she said: "Why don't you call first."

Dangling from her key chain was a fur pom-pom, identical to the ones attached to the gloves in her hand and on her cropped down jacket.

"He's not home, so—"

"My phone's not working," she interrupted.

She left the stroller in the hall and entered with Dream, even though Therese hadn't invited her in.

"Lucky for you I showed up," she said. "How long have you been sitting there?"

She didn't answer.

"Where's Alex?" she asked.

"Don't know, but he won't be back right away."

"Okay."

They lingered in the hall.

She looked at her reflection in the mirror on the wall, her bruised cheek. Dream had scuttled into the living room and pulled herself up on the coffee table. She was balancing on its edges, toddling back and forth, shaking with laughter.

Therese wasn't paying attention to Dream, neither did she mention what happened the night before, she simply walked out onto the balcony.

She followed, leaving the door ajar.

"It's like this," Therese said, and gestured to the living room where daylight was mingling with the dark. "Alex has what he needs to do his job. It's not like he's sitting on a bunch of capital." She lit a cigarette.

"You had it fucking made, Karin," she continued. "Better than most of us. Why don't you look at it that way? Or is that too hard?"

She didn't know what to say.

Of course, Therese was right.

She searched through all that was drifting around inside her. Therese wasn't going to make apologies for Alex, that much was clear. She reminded herself to be smart. Don't cry. Don't talk about old times, when they were getting to know John and Alex and everybody else. Or before. And don't get desperate and try to win her over.

They went inside.

Dream was sitting on the floor, staring at her hands. The child took no notice of them.

She sat on the sofa, still dressed in her layers. Therese plopped herself down in the swiveling armchair, took out a baggie, and tipped a measure of cocaine on a gossip magazine on the table. She bent over the glossy, cut the powder into two thin lines, and snorted one.

"So what now, Karin?" she asked, sniffing to make sure it all went in. "You need me to watch her again?"

She didn't reply and reached for the banknote Therese had used and snorted the other line. Her sinuses felt cold and clear.

"I still think there's a stash that belongs to me," she said. "That should be mine. And hers."

Therese lit a cigarette and rolled her eyes.

It was a punch to the gut. She'd become one of *those* people. The ones they meant when they used to say to each other: "At least *we* didn't get knocked up." They'd always drawn a line between themselves and the bitches who dragged innocent children into the game because they couldn't resist giving in to their biological urges. And here she was using a kid she'd brought into this world—with her eyes wide open—as a justification for why she was entitled to something that might not even exist.

"If it were only me I wouldn't care," she said, "but you know . . . for her sake. I want my money, and I want her to have what's rightfully hers." She could hear how she sounded.

Therese's jaw dropped; she looked squarely at Dream, and then out the window before slapping the table so hard a plastic container fell over and bottles of nail polish rolled out.

"Goddamnit!" she screamed. The cigarette flew from her hand.

Dream started crying.

She took her baby in her arms and gathered up the nail polish, heart racing.

Therese reached for the cigarette, which left a burn mark on the grimy linoleum floor, and took a quick drag.

"Why are you doing this to me? Why are you putting me in this position?" she seethed. "It's not like you." Therese got up, shook her head, and glared at her. "I don't know what's going on in your head. You think you're immune? Do you still think you're above it all, and you can do whatever you want and no one can touch you?"

She avoided Therese's eyes by looking at Dream, who had quieted down and was nestled in her arms, face against her breast.

"I mean, look at you!" Therese screamed. "You have. A fucking. Child."

She was struggling to hold back her tears, and she couldn't decide if it would be bad or good to cry in front of Therese.

She said:

"But don't you think it's a shame?"

Therese pressed her lips together and sucked on her teeth. She nodded a few times, wiped her nose with her hand, and sniffed. She looked as if she was trying to keep from hitting someone.

"What's a shame?" she asked. "You mean you and me?"

"Yes." A tear rolled down her cheek. "I hadn't even met John yet when you and I became friends."

"Sure, Karin, but what the fuck? That's exactly why I'm telling you to get it together. Anything can happen, you know that. We're not fucking around here."

She nodded. "Right," she said. "I know."

"And you've got nothing. You're all alone."

"I know."

She just sat there.

Therese cursed and walked out of the room.

She stayed put, tears streaming down her face, and rested her hand on Dream's back, wishing that the peace the child seemed to possess in spite of everything would be transmitted through her palm.

Before she left, she called to Therese. Once.

Outside the building, mothers carrying grocery bags and children made their way through the courtyard, heads bowed in the wind that doubled in strength as it channeled between the high-rise apartments. A gust snatched her hair from her jacket, and in the underpass that led to the center of town another gust whipped up flurries of sand from the dry ground, as if it weren't winter at all. She covered her face with her arm and ran through the tunnel, blinking and spitting. On the other side, she crouched down in front of the stroller. Her eyes burned and her mouth was gritty.

Dream was sleeping, undisturbed.

Gently, she brushed the sand off Dream's cheeks, stood up, and carried on. She took the elevator down to the subway platform, ran to catch the train, and made it, just. She parked the stroller and found a seat. The effects of the cocaine were waning, and she felt groggy again, loose and granular.

She rested her head against the window.

The glass juddered when the train began to move. Through darkness and light, past snowy parks and soccer fields, residential neighborhoods sprouting from the loam of the road system. As it flew along the wet, rugged walls of mountain passages, concrete tunnels strung with wires, lined with beams, rippled beside her like a hot wave.

A T THE subway entrance, workers were spraying a hot water solution on the thick ice covering the stairs. She pushed Dream's stroller up a slippery steel track ramp that ran along the wall. The glycol in the air irritated her eyes and she tried to press one of her ears against her shoulder to block out the sound of shovels scraping the rough tiles.

People flowed past her on their way into and out of the subway, pushing and crowding in the center of the steps to avoid the spray from the water jets. She gripped the ice-cold metal railing with her left hand. With her right, she held one stroller handle, and tried to maneuver the other with her elbow. Crooked and stooped, she guided the stroller up the ramp. Moving carefully, she focused her energy on reaching the top.

Halfway there, the stroller suddenly felt heavier. She was losing control and had to take a step down. And then another. The wet gravel grating under her shoes set her teeth on edge. The stroller slipped toward her. She stopped, unable to move, afraid of losing her balance. Behind her, people who also wanted to use the ramp as a shortcut were harrumphing. Soon another woman with a stroller appeared.

She tightened her grip on the railing.

She was sweating and dragging herself forward, forcing herself not to worry about slipping, spurring herself on. A man ducked under the railing that separated the ramp from the steps and grabbed one of the handles. It was over in a flash. Working together, they reached the top, and then they were on the landing. The sky was a lid, containing everything outside.

"Thank you," she said.

He reached out his hand and at first she didn't understand; she didn't need any more help.

"Please," he said.

His open hand, the coal-black lines of his palm, was extended between them.

She shook her head and walked down the sidewalk, pushing Dream across a square with a parking structure, a few fast-food stands on one side, and an ice-skating rink with pitted ice on the other. Exhaust fumes and hot dogs. She tensed in an attempt to keep the cold at bay and set her jaw to quiet the shudders running along her spine. There seemed to be no barrier between her and the outside world—wide open, windblown.

She waited at the intersection's crosswalk like everyone else—around her swarms of people stalked through the cold wearing dogged expressions—and when she stepped onto the street she glanced up at the roofs. Anything was possible.

Finally, she was ready to take action.

She saw Alex, Therese, and Abbe in the clouds. Unflinching. Chieftains who had expelled her from the tribe. People changed depending on where you were in relation to them—how close or far. The circle changes when you're on the outside.

She hadn't heard from Abbe in months.

A woman biked leisurely across the street, pushing two children in the cart in front of her. A teddy bear was propped up in the basket. The clouds overhead had begun to move.

She started walking.

The tips of her ankle boots were streaked with salt, and water was seeping in and soaking her toes. The stroller's wheels skidded in the snow-soup and Dream was babbling melodically.

How long had she been doing that?

She wanted to let her know that she'd heard her, but didn't have the energy to reach around the canopy and communicate with the child. On the street were slender pieces of dog shit, and farther ahead, the sidewalk was cordoned off with traffic cones and plastic tape whipping in the wind.

She was startled by snow falling from the roof of the building closest to her. She looked up and saw some men moving around, dislodging sheets of snow and ice and shouting at each other in a language she didn't recognize.

Their shovels scraped and the snow rumbled as it slid across the sheet-metal roofs and fell to the ground. Billows of ice flakes scattered in the wind and the hard chunks bounced and shattered when they landed on the pavement, dusting it with snow.

In the middle of the street was a young man with flaming red ears and a whistle. He looked at her and signaled with the whistle, a brief blast; the men on the roof stopped their shoveling. Silence. When she had passed them, the man whistled a second time and the men went back to work.

Dream was making her singing sounds again.

He was the one who'd wanted to have a child, but she was the one who'd had her. She was the one who was here now, trudging through the snow with the stroller. This is what he'd left her. There was nothing else. No house to sell, no cash, no money in the accounts, not even in the one with the long number she'd memorized. The one she was supposed to be able to access under circumstances like these. When everything had gone to hell.

ON THE side streets, the snow was sooty and muddy, and slush covered the pavement. Snowed-over cars crowded the curb. In front of her, a man holding an empty plastic bag slipped; the wind puffed out his quilted jacket. The stench of hair and dried urine moved through the cold air as he passed by—so pungent it seemed to reach out and touch her.

She gagged.

Stopped, swallowed, let go of the stroller, leaned against the building, and breathed through her nose. She searched her pockets for the cigarettes and lighter, found them, lit up, and stuffed a piece of gum into her mouth.

She passed the gym where she and Therese used to work out, continued on through a small park with swings and benches, and when she came out on the other side she was on Abbe's street. Narrow and dark, even though it was daytime. The snowy sidewalk was strewn with trash. The building was plastered with posters and the marks they left behind after they'd been torn off.

She arrived at a door, certain it was his, but unsure if she'd find him at home. He might not even live there anymore.

He hadn't been in contact since Dream was born and who knows? Maybe he'd try to scare her off as Alex had, or worse, and yet he was the only person she dared hang any hope on. Yes, that's what she was feeling: a kind of reinvigorated hope.

She typed in the door code. It didn't work.

She glanced over her shoulder. It wouldn't be good if he showed up now. If she was going to ask for help, she'd have to surprise him. She'd have to gauge his reaction when he first laid eyes on her; he shouldn't have a chance to plan his response.

She crossed the street and stood outside a boutique, a clothing-shop-cum-nail-salon. A girl was crouched on the floor, playing with a small dog that was jumping up and down. The door was open a crack in spite of the weather, and just inside was an old-fashioned cash register. Next to the flyers stacked on the sill of the bay window, a cell phone was charging. Anyone could reach in and snatch it.

You could take the whole register, but there probably wasn't much in it anyway. How much did homegirl earn for sitting around? Was it her store? Maybe she didn't even need the money, maybe she was working just to have something to do.

She looked at a pair of shoes in the window. The pretty pale leather on the inside would go gray as soon as someone started wearing them. The girl caught sight of her, and she turned to face the street; she looked up at what she thought was Abbe's window.

Dead.

The front door of the building opened. A woman in a sweat suit appeared. She zipped across the street with the stroller, but by the time she reached the door, it had already shut.

She was out of breath.

"Do you have the code?"

The woman looked her up and down.

"I'm sorry," she said. "We never give it out."

"But my friend lives here, and I know the old one. 3647!"

She tried a casual smile, but the woman shook her head and waved as she jogged off. "Sorry!"

Her shoes were wet.

She climbed onto the stoop and took a quick look around. Then she cupped her hands over the keypad, pressed her mouth to her thumbs, and exhaled audibly between them. Even though she was so cold, the air coming out of her was hot, and when she took her hands away and leaned in for a closer look, two keys were less fogged than the others. She blew on them again, focused, and kept going until another two keys stood out. The effort made her dizzy and she steadied herself against the door, took a deep breath, straightened up, and started pressing the four buttons in various combinations until she heard the door unlock with a click.

The stairwell was dark and silent. She'd parked the stroller and was climbing the stairs with Dream when she heard an unsettling sound. A nervous smacking. She quickly realized it was coming from her own mouth. Now that she was thinking about it, the gum was like cold plastic.

She spit it out.

On the third floor, she saw his name on the door. Leaving herself no room for hesitation, she rang the bell.

It was a normal door. With a normal lock. A peephole.

She kept her head down, so he wouldn't be able to tell it was her right away; he might think it was a neighbor with her baby.

But no one answered.

She lingered there until Dream started crying. Then she sat on the stairs, on the second step from the bottom, and offered Dream her breast, cradling her tiny, hot body. Her mind thickened as the baby fed.

The stairwell smelled of stone and cement, scents she'd loved during her pregnancy. Baseboards framed the stone tile floor. People had been wandering through this place for more than a century. Perhaps they'd faced equally unpredictable situations. It's never the first time for anything.

Dream had emptied both of her breasts and let out a substantial burp. Still, no one had come or gone, and she hadn't heard anyone at the front door. It was silent but for the sound of Dream breathing through her nose as she drifted off to sleep. The child's cheeks were supple, frost-nipped. The breast-feeding had worn her out too; she should have brought a bottle of water from home.

She leaned her head against the wall, and looked at the solid dark-wood doors and the brass name plaques and various notices declaring that the residents did not wish to receive junk mail. She imagined what the apartments looked like on the inside and who lived here.

When she was pregnant, he'd talked about them going away. He'd wanted to leave everything behind, and the thought had filled her with an effervescent heat, like falling in love with him all over again.

He wanted nothing but her.

Now she understood why she'd cherished that fantasy. It had given her hope. Even then she must have known, somewhere deep down, that she was actually on her own.

She nodded off, head against the wall, and came to a bit later, convinced she'd dropped Dream on the floor. When she opened her eyes, the child was still dozing in her arms. Lips parted, glistening within.

She was thirsty and had to pee.

She tried to move her feet, but her legs had fallen asleep, so she sat there yawning and making small, careful movements, waiting for the sensation to return. As she got up, her hair caught in the railing, and her yelp woke Dream.

The front door opened.

She tried to hush the baby.

A few hairs were stuck in the bracket; dangling there, they looked like a crack in the wall.

She listened to the person climb the stairs and stop one floor below. A door was unlocked, opened, and shut.

He might not be back before the evening.

She held Dream until she reached the bottom of the stairs, where she put her in the stroller and walked out to the street.

THE AIR was hazy and the snow clouds seemed to want to drag the sky to the ground. She kept both hands on the stroller and looked at the street. Cobblestones stuck out from holes in the ice, and the rivulets of meltwater would soon freeze again. Thick ice hung from the pipes.

She turned a corner, slipped past a stalled plow parked with its emergency lights blinking, and hurried over to the gym in the large brick building.

The restroom was right by the entrance. Inside, the scent of a pungent air freshener hit her. She was about to wet herself, and yet managed to fling open the door and lock it behind her while balancing unsteadily on her toes and squeezing her knees together. She hobbled back toward the toilet, dress gathered in one hand, tugged her stockings and panties down, and tumbled onto the seat.

Relief.

She wanted to drain herself, and never have to use the toilet ever again.

When she was finished, she took the opportunity to change Dream on a changing table even though it wasn't really necessary. Then she tucked her into the bunting bag and washed her hands, rocking the stroller with one foot. She ran her fingers through her hair, spit on a paper towel, and wiped flecks of mascara from under her eyes.

The day care was at the end of the hallway beyond the restroom.

She parked her stroller with the others and sat on a bench for a while with Dream on her lap.

There was a radiator under the bench, and she leaned back and basked in the heat, an electric heat that encouraged her to relax and doze off. Mothers holding their children walked past, yoga mats slung over their shoulders, and she couldn't help staring at their bodies: the veins running down their arms, their lean muscles. She shut her eyes to avoid eye contact and to keep from seeing their open, clean faces.

Outside the gym, she took out a cigarette. She stayed close to the wall, sheltered by the overhang, and tried to light it. A cracking sound came from above. She caught sight of a large icicle dropping from the roof. It shattered right beside her.

She stared at the shards, stunned. Falling ice could be fatal.

She cupped her hand over her cigarette and managed to light it.

What would happen to Dream if an icicle smashed into her head?

As she walked away with the stroller, a man approached her.

Her first impulse was to run, but she skidded along in her ankle boots while replaying what she'd said to Therese and to the lawyer. She couldn't think of anyone who might be after her because of what she'd told them.

When she looked up, he was next to her.

She stopped.

The man lunged forward, swatting at the cigarette. She stepped back and jerked her hand away, but he managed to land a blow and the cigarette fell to the ground.

"You shouldn't be smoking!" he shouted.

"Excuse me?"

"Are you *trying* to poison your child?" He pointed at Dream, who was fast asleep. His voice echoed between the buildings.

No cars drove by; barely a soul was around. A woman with a cane on the other side of the street was staring at them.

Silence.

She noticed her mouth hanging open, so she shut it. He looked at the cigarette soaking in the slush, glanced at her, and walked out into the street; he stumbled over a dog piss- and tobacco-stained snowbank and disappeared down the road.

She walked away, fast.

She lit another cigarette.

A flaming blush spread from her cheeks across her face, to her ears and the back of her neck.

Is this what everyone expected to happen? Had she been the last to notice she was heading in this direction? She'd never really seen through the lies. She felt his contempt when he talked about strategies and plans. His eyes would smolder—a glow that appeared when he was high on himself, his unsurpassed power and ability to fuck the system time after time. But she had believed him when he said she'd never have to live without him unless she wanted to.

When they were together, she trusted him implicitly. When she had doubts, all she had to do was nestle into him until his words and silences became her own, and everything he said sounded true.

She passed an old factory that had been converted into a restaurant. Her lips were sore. She pulled at a piece of dry skin with her front teeth, peeling it off slowly so as not to tear the flesh, and swallowed it. She licked her lips, chapped and raw from the cold winter air.

She caught a glimpse of the former factory's large interior courtyard. In its center, the cobblestones had been replaced by a soft material, padding for a jungle gym. Children swaddled in bulky winter gear were playing while their parents, wrapped in blankets under large heat lamps, sat drinking beer and champagne.

Ambling by, she peered through the windows of the large deli and restaurant and caught her reflection in the glass separating her from the people indulging in late lunches with wine, or others working hard, computers and coffee cups arranged in front of them. In the delicatessen were freshly baked cinnamon buns and croissants; air-cured ham was suspended above the counter. A woman her age was holding a basket of fresh herbs and chatting to the shop assistant while her little girl was lining up yellow lemons on the conveyor belt at the check-out counter.

She must have looked like an idiot, standing there and staring. But nobody was paying attention to her.

She tried to remember who she'd once been, tried to convince herself that a trace of that person was still inside her.

She walked on.

ABBE'S BODY seemed to take up the entire doorway. Either she wasn't remembering him properly or he had gotten even bigger. His eye mask was pushed up on his forehead and he was holding a book in one hand, a thick, well-thumbed paperback copy of *Shantaram*, which he set on the shelf of the coatrack without taking his eyes off her.

He just stood there, looking at her. She couldn't read any animosity in his face, but the silence was long enough to make her wonder if he was going to smack her too, if she should turn around and go.

"Looky here," he said. "It's Karin."

He smiled to himself, his gaze hazy.

"Hi," she said.

Holding Dream, she took a step toward him, and he hugged them both as though they might break.

"Hey lady," he said. "And little lady."

His large hand patted Dream's head.

And then they went inside the apartment.

He looked at the baby and at her, laughed, and shook his head.

She felt herself smiling.

"Did we wake you?" she asked.

"No, no."

He shrugged and led the way into the kitchen. He was dressed as usual: track pants and plastic slide sandals, as if he were doing time. One side of his neck was adorned with leaves and barbed wire; a phoenix was rising up from his chest. His skin was covered in ink, but he wasn't like every bro who was copying this look nowadays: she knew each tattoo still meant something to him.

"Long time, Karin."

He seemed surprised, but that was all.

She tried to give him another smile.

The apartment was empty but for a sofa, apparently brand new, and a large television. On the floor in front of it lay a pile of video-game controls and cables. In the kitchen, two incense cones had turned to ash on one of the burners. On the windowsill was a row of cell phones. In front of each was a piece of masking tape covered in notes made with a felt-tip pen.

A small black plastic coffeemaker was sitting in the middle of the kitchen counter. While he made coffee, she stood by the window, taking in the telephones and the snowy rooftops outside. It was warm over by the radiator, and her body quaked as the electric heat reached into her frozen core.

He didn't notice.

On the nearest roof, several men were shoveling snow. They had secured themselves with a rope fastened to a chimney and were gesturing to each other as they went back and forth. White clouds of breath floated among them.

She turned and caught him looking at her.

She wondered what he was thinking. She didn't know much about him. And nothing about who he was when she was on her own. When John wasn't around.

"Just so you know, I'm outta milk," he said.

"No problem."

He smiled; his large hands fumbled as he placed the coffee pods in the machine one at a time, and brewed them each a cup.

They sat on the sofa, facing each other. The coffee was hot and she didn't want to wait for it to cool, so it scalded her tongue as she drank, but even that didn't warm her up. He had two of those mugs with Nicholas's picture on them. Both as chipped and worn as hers. Dream sat on the rug in the hallway, playing with one of his large shoes, trying to fit it into her mouth, covering it in drool. She got up, took it away from her, and gave her the rubber giraffe instead.

Abbe's coffee mug was resting against his track pants, black with white stripes running down the sides. His lap looked as though it would make a nice pillow.

"What's up?" he asked.

She shrugged and shook her head.

"Karin, you think too much. This isn't the first time I'm telling you. Don't think so much. Talk to me instead."

He patted the sofa next to him.

"Have you met someone?" he asked after she sat back down.

"No, of course not," she shot back.

She felt walls go up around her. She sensed a familiar threat, which gave rise to that faint buzzing sensation. As if she were something of value, rather than a prisoner.

Still, it surprised her that he hadn't hesitated to ask. That there wasn't anything else he wanted to say first.

"Oh shit," he said. "Sorry."

"I haven't been up to much of anything," she said.

She looked at him and sighed.

He grabbed her shoulders, hugged her briefly. Shaking his head, he held her out in front of him as if he couldn't believe she was really there and smiled in a way that allowed her to muster a smile for him.

"It's fuckin' rad seeing the little lady too," he said, and cleared his throat.

She nodded.

"Dream," she said.

"Right. Dream. I knew that."

Yes, he absolutely did.

She got up and went into the kitchen, where Dream was trying to pull out a drawer. She picked her up and took a spin around Abbe's apartment, showing her the view over the narrow street and the cars and the boutique across the way. She put Dream in Abbe's lap. He tickled her neck and tummy with his large fingers.

"This little piggy went to market. This little piggy stayed home . . ."

When he paused, Dream opened her eyes wide with an anticipation that surprised her—they'd never played like that—and then he kept walking his fingers over her body:

"This little piggy had roast beef . . ."

Pause.

"This little piggy had none . . ."

He tickled her harder on her neck and chin and his voice rose higher and higher until he was squealing.

"And this little piggy went wee wee wee all the way home."

Dream shook with laughter and Abbe caught the drool spilling from her mouth with his index finger. He put the child down next to her on the sofa, got up, and went to the kitchen.

She heard him open the refrigerator, set the microwave, open and close some cabinets. There was a "ding." The smell of saffron and dried lime filled the small apartment and he returned, his large hands full, balancing two plates of rice and stew and two glasses. Under his arm was a bottle of low-calorie juice, which he placed on the coffee table.

"I'm all about cooking in bulk now," he said. "So there's always something to eat at home. This shit gets better when it's reheated." She downed her juice and he refilled the glass.

She asked for water and he brought her some.

"Does she need a plate?"

"Oh, no. No, she doesn't eat solid foods yet."

"But you've let her taste, right?" he called from the kitchen.

She thought about it.

"No."

"You should. Otherwise you won't know what she'll want when it's time for her to start."

He came back into the room with a piece of bread that he put in Dream's hand. He dipped his pinky in the warm stew, which was dotted with glossy fat, and carefully stuck it in her little mouth. She didn't seem to understand what he wanted her to do.

They ate in silence. Plates in their laps, shoveling food into their mouths, not looking at each other. The sauce ran down her chin and she wiped it away with her hand without his noticing. The water helped her wash down the pieces of okra and salty chicken, which she practically swallowed whole. Heat spread through her body as she ate and watched Dream, who was slumped against a cushion on the sofa, holding her crust of bread.

Abbe set down his plate and leaned back and burped. He closed his eyes, placed his hand on her knee, and then looked at her.

"I don't know what to say, Karin. I know you're tough, but, well . . . It's nice seeing you."

Tears.

She hadn't planned on crying.

Hiding her face, she found a place to put her plate, curled up on her side, and rested her head on his lap. She felt his hand on her back. He began to stroke her; she could've stayed like that forever. Under the weight of his hot hand.

She felt as if she'd been trekking across an icy expanse, and this was the destination.

She could have fallen asleep right there in his lap and not woken up for hours.

Her head was heavy, her body was heavy. But she pulled herself together, focused on the cables on the floor in front of the television, and forced herself to wake up, moving one hand to his leg and gently poking his knee.

"Hey," she said. "Who should I talk to about money?"

Abbe took a deep breath and sighed. Exhaling through his nose. He slowly bowed his head, gripped her hair, and tilted her face toward his.

She didn't open her eyes.

"I mean, John's cut of your last job together," she said. "I'd like to have that cut."

"Huh?"

She looked at him. First he was expressionless, then surprised.

"What are you talking about?"

She sat up.

"Abbe," she said. "I'm freaking out." She took the paper from her jacket, which lay on the sofa; unfolded it; and handed it to him. "They're taking the house."

He read it. Then looked at her.

"They've sicced the Enforcement Authority on me and everything."

"Shit."

"Yeah."

He put the paper on the table.

She could feel the heat of his stare.

"Why the fuck did they do that?"

She shrugged. Trying to dodge the worry that flitted through her. The all-encompassing worry they imparted with their letters and inquiries and visits.

"Fucking pigs," he said.

He lit a cigarette and waved it in the air.

"It's like, they're like—" he said. "They're taking our basic fucking rights away."

He spoke slowly. Pauses punctuated the words; he articulated each and every one.

"Yo, that's all we are to them. Third-class citizens. Or not even. Why should we go straight, when they take what you've got, and what your family's got, no matter how you roll."

He ashed on the plate.

She lay back down in his lap and looked out at the sky.

Motionless.

She heard John in each of his words and his body heat made her feel that she belonged and had arrived.

"You can always get another house," he said. "Who knows? It might end up you and me, babe!"

He let out one of his rare childish laughs, and she laughed too, not because it was funny but to let him know that they were friends, and he was allowed to joke around with her, and then she heard John's sternest voice inside her, that unyielding titanium and diamond tone.

"When the cat's away, Karin," it said.

She shook her head and laughed some more.

Abbe grinned.

She wondered what he could offer her.

"Thing is, he'd be cool with us. But you know that."

She pretended she hadn't heard him.

"For real, Abbe. I have to do something," she said, sitting up. "They're even taking the car. I don't have anywhere to live. No cash. No wheels. Nothing."

It was hard to make this sound like anything but a line. But she knew he was hearing the words as she'd intended them. He knew all about people without means; it was a familiar story. He wouldn't think she was lying.

"Shit, babe," he said.

He hugged her and then made her lie down again.

"Oh man, I was supposed to have your back."

"Yeah, you messed that up, didn't you? You and everyone else."

She spoke into his lap.

She shut her eyes and wished she'd stop existing. She wished to be released from her burdens.

"I mean, I get it, no one has anyone's back," she went on. "All that talk about being there for each other, it's bullshit. I know that now, so I'm not taking it personally."

"But—"

"Seriously, come on. No one *actually* cares about anyone else. It's obvious. It's just a way to hold on to the feeling that what we have is valuable because we have this bond, even though we don't, really."

He rubbed his face and then his eye.

"Hold up, Karin. It's not like you made it fuckin' easy for us. You try getting into that fortress of yours out there."

She shut her eyes. He ran his fingers through her hair and mussed it, strands snagged in the grooves of his dry fingertips. He tucked her hair behind her ear.

"Karin, I'm sorry," he said. His hot hand lingered, as if he couldn't help himself. "I wish I could fix this for you. Honest."

She looked ahead without saying a word.

She pursed her lips and curled up tightly.

"I'll think about it," he said, and put a hand on her shoulder. "You hear me?"

She didn't reply, but stared coldly into the room.

His hand on her shoulder, a hesitant kneading. She swallowed. Her cheek on his faded pants. An airy feeling.

"Damn girl, you're tense."

He massaged her shoulder and the back of her neck.

"It's the breast-feeding," she said softly. "It's all shoulders and back."

He hummed and nodded, working her shoulders with his thumbs, so hard it hurt, but the muscles began to yield and the blood flooded through new channels.

She sank deeper and deeper, down into his lap.

The darkness inside her was warm. Night moons and day moons rose and set in concert. She let herself fall into blackness, across the world, around it, around the moons. Alone.

His fingers moved along her neck.

She heard him say that it was as hard as fucking stone and she heard his fingers in her hair, the strands rubbing against each other between his rough fingertips and the silky skin at the nape of her neck. Halfheartedly, she lifted her head and said:

"Who should I talk to, Abbe? Forget about then, help me now."

He looked down at her.

He took hold of her shoulders again and gently pressed her collarbone with his thumb. How easily he could break her, snap the bone. He smiled sweetly, as if it were a friendly touch.

"Babe, you're not gonna talk to anyone. Got it?"

She sat up.

He shoved his hand into his pocket. Put a stack of cash on the coffee table. "We're family. If you need money, you come to me."

She didn't move.

He pointed at the table.

She looked between the money and him.

She took the money only because he jutted his head forward and opened his eyes wide. She placed the stack in her lap and wrapped her hands around it. She smiled at him and realized it was because she felt afraid.

He smiled back. Calmer now.

He reached for her and played with the hair falling over her shoulder, studied the pale wisps between his fingers. She suspected he was enjoying the feeling of being her daddy now, how pleased he was that she wanted him to take care of her.

"Thank you," she said, gripping the bills. "But you do understand, I need my own money."

"Karin," he said.

Her name, that was all, but that one word bore a litany of admonitions, requests. Rules.

"You need something, it's yours. You need a phone?"

She didn't answer.

He reached past her and picked up a couple of keys from the table, a worn Marlboro key ring.

"Here." He held them out in front of her. "This is your place now."

She hesitated.

"You two can take my room, and I'll sleep here."

He patted the sofa.

She didn't say a word.

"No, not like that, Karin! No, no, no. I won't bother you. I'm always gone!"

She had to keep from rolling her eyes, and a sigh escaped instead.

"Have you sold any of the stuff at the house?" he asked.

"No. Just my purses and whatever. Nothing else."

His steady gaze.

"But I guess I should."

"I can help if you need me to," he said. "Bring your stuff here before they get their hands on it."

"Sure. Great. But I still need my cut."

She put the money back on the coffee table.

He sighed, stroked his face, and looked at her. She knew what he was thinking. He thought she was the kind of person who needed money a little more than everyone else did, but she took care not to mention it.

"I don't *know* anything," she said. "But I know some cunt is holding on to it. If they cared about John at all, they would've already given me my share."

He pressed his palms against his eyes.

"All right. I'll handle it," he said. "You're right. Obviously. We'll figure something out. Something that's good for you and for her. I'll do some thinking. Don't worry."

"What do you mean?"

"Trust. I'll have a word with Alex."

She threw herself over him. She couldn't believe her ears, it felt like old times, as if John was back.

"Thank you!" she said.

She pressed her face against his chest; it was rock hard, even harder than she'd imagined. As if he were wearing a vest. She glanced at his neck and shoulders, the contours of his body under his sweater. Then she sat up and looked around for Dream, listened for noises, and heard her fiddling with a kitchen drawer again.

She let herself fall into him, her face against his chest. His hands ran up and down her back and she felt herself thaw, quieting down inside.

"I know you want it," he said, and grabbed her upper thigh, hard.

"No," she replied.

S HE MADE her way down the street, feeling that each pass-erby was looking right through her, as though John were watching her, and she was ashamed, ashamed of what she'd wanted to do and still wanted to do. Quaking and longing, the thoughts she'd had.

That simpleminded body against hers.

She wound through the one-way side streets in Abbe's neighborhood—tattoo parlors, clothing shops, small bars not open yet—and emerged on a larger street. Along one side ran a jet-black cliff face. Ice hung from the granite shelves like white beards, ragged and yellow on the surface, blue and spar-kling, quartz-like within. On the other side was an apartment building, covered in scrawled tags and grimy with exhaust.

She guided the stroller down the sidewalk, shoving it through the snow. They reached a small square at the end of the rocky rise. A movement caught her eye; a rat dashed across one of the benches, leapt onto the ground, and disap-peared into a hole under a cluster of thorny bushes at the foot of the hill.

If you believe everything will turn out okay, will it? Or should you not tempt fate and believe that nothing will go your way, like an incantation?

She crossed the wide street, where there was a bend in the road and a low stone wall running along one side. She parked the stroller next to it and lit a cigarette. The tobacco had fallen out of the tip. The flame devoured the paper as soon as it caught fire.

It was a mighty view and the sky above was endless. No longer a leaden gray. Where the clouds had parted, the heavens were streaked with hazy pastel rays. The wind rolling over the sea whipped her face and made her eyes water; her tears were shining shards filtering the view of the city below. Churches and commercial skyscrapers, a palace and a medieval city center, traffic meandering over bridges. Smoke rose from tall chimneys, and large, dark channels had been carved between the ice floes; a couple of small boats and a passenger ferry sailed toward a cruise ship waiting in the distance.

In the low wall were evenly spaced embrasures for the cannons that had once protected the city from attacks by sea. On the capstones snow—now hard-packed—had settled in the recesses of the granite, and its surface was porous and wet. She placed her red hands on the snow, leaned over the wall, and looked down; if she fell, it would hurt. Her body would slam against the stones protruding from the cliff before it hit the ground.

It was a straight drop to the highway; between the road and the rock wall, something was moving. Dark spots, like bacteria under a microscope. She could make out a pile of black trash bags partly buried in snow and realized the spots were rats, scurrying.

Dream was awake and looking straight ahead, bright-eyed. She bent forward and tightened the hood around her face and straightened out the bunting bag. Her breasts were swollen. Heavy and hard, chafing against her armpits even though it hadn't been long since the last feeding.

It must be the weather, she thought.

When winter was over, it would be better.

She flicked her cigarette and thought she saw it land by the trash. Then she walked until she reached a bus stop. When the bus arrived, she climbed on at the back and squeezed into the space designated for strollers. She wasn't going far.

THE SMALL café had a large window that faced the street. She parked the stroller outside and noticed she was gnashing her gum again. Nerves.

She spit it out and went inside.

Anna had done the place up. The walls were stripped to the plaster, the same shade as the concrete floor, and the menu had been scribbled right on one wall in chalk. At the bar were a shiny juicer and a crate full of fruits and vegetables. There didn't appear to be any customers, but someone, maybe Anna, was moving around behind a curtain hung in the doorway behind the bar.

She cleared her throat.

The curtain was pushed aside.

A man appeared. She didn't see anyone behind him.

"Is Anna around?" she asked.

"No."

"But she works here, right?"

"Sure, but not today. She's at home."

"Do you think I could give her a call?"

"Go right ahead."

"I mean, could I use your phone?"

He took out his cell phone and handed it to her; it was already ringing. She sat down by the window and watched

Dream sleep in her stroller. The guy leaned on the bar, watching her every move. And then she heard Anna's voice:

"I already told you, I'm not coming in today!"

"Sorry," she said. "It's me, Karin. I'm at your work."

Silence.

"Hello?" she asked. "Anna?"

Nothing.

A distant "Yeah" materialized. "Hey. What do you want?"

"I just wanted to catch up, so I stopped by. I brought Dream too . . . I've got a situation."

"I know. I heard. Therese told me."

"Oh, right. So you guys are hanging out like always?"

"Yeah."

"Okay." She looked at the concrete floor. "Do you think we could maybe get together? I could swing by your place, and then you'd get to see Dream. She's gotten so big so fast."

She heard Anna take a deep breath.

"Karin, I'm not sure that's such a good idea," she said. "I mean, what happened to you fucking sucks, but I don't think there's anything I can do about it. Right? Understand?"

She was speechless.

She heard a child shouting in the background and waited for Anna to say something else, but the call ended.

The guy had come out from behind the bar and was standing right next to her, as if he expected her to make a run for it with his phone. She got up.

She said "Thanks" without looking at him, put the phone on the bar, and walked out.

THE AFTERNOON light cast wide blue streaks across the snow and street. Dream was still sleeping in the stroller. She undid the brake, and just as she was about to leave, she found herself in someone's way, excused herself, and looked up.

It was Therese, on her way to Anna's. She stopped in mid-step and stared at her.

"What are you doing here?" she asked.

"I was at Abbe's, so I thought I'd stop by. But she's not in today."

Therese didn't move.

"What were you and Abbe doing?"

"Nothing. He gave me the keys to his place. He's going to help me out."

"Oh really."

She nodded.

Therese laughed.

"What?"

"Don't get me wrong, I'm not dissing John," she said, "but maybe he didn't always have the full picture. He might not've been as on the ball as you guys thought."

"What do you mean?"

"Come on. Think about it."

Therese looked around and said:

"You still think he's so smart and that everyone admires him. Don't you? That's sweet, really it is. But you know . . . There are two sides to everything."

"All right," she said. "What are you trying to say?"

"I mean, think about Abbe and Alex. He was, like, the leader for so long, and they're all friends . . ." She spoke slowly, searchingly, watching her all the while, as if she didn't want to miss her reaction. "I don't know. Maybe it was eating away at them. It's as simple as that, I guess. It's not like they kept me in the loop."

"What are you talking about?"

"Don't you get it?" Therese laughed. "Oh my god, I can't help it. You're just so fucking—" She cut herself off. Shook her head, closed her eyes, and covered her temples with her hands.

"They screwed him over," she exclaimed with a look that bordered on triumphant.

She couldn't breathe, couldn't speak.

Finally she managed to say: "Why didn't you tell me?"

"Why would I? You haven't exactly been available. But I'm telling you now, aren't I?"

The ground fell away from under her feet, taking her body with it.

Everything was as nothing.

"So I probably wouldn't put all my trust in Abbe if I were you," Therese continued, watching her as she sank onto a ledge protruding from the building. "And it's no secret that Alex isn't exactly happy about you dropping by and asking for help."

"What the fuck am I supposed to do?"

"Dunno." Therese sat down next to her. She pulled her hair to one side and when the light from the café spilled over her, a dark shadow appeared. Bruises dappled the side of her face and part of her neck. "I mean, whatever it is you want, take it."

T HE SURGING rage. It put a twitch in her movements, turned her thoughts black, and made them impenetrable. She passed the katsuras and the roundabout. Most of the journey was behind her. It wasn't far now. She'd be home soon, even though "home" no longer felt like the right word for it. And technically, it wasn't.

She dragged the stroller over the snowbanks marking the border between the street and the vast wintery field, and rolled it through the snow until it wouldn't roll any more. She parked Dream and walked toward the crab apple tree, its gnarled branches caked in white. Throbbing and stumbling, she sprinted the last few feet, the snow at her calves.

When she reached the tree, she paused to glance over her shoulder.

The road was as empty as before.

The stroller was a phantom in the white. All was still.

She worked her foot out of the snow and kicked the black tree trunk. Snow dropped from the branches, right onto her, but she didn't flinch. She kicked and kicked, and noticed that she was fully aware of what was happening, how she was permitting herself to unload on the tree. Her aggression wasn't wild. She slapped the trunk. Each blow, each kick was intentional, and she kept at it until she missed and tore a gash across her hand.

It stung and glistened. She made a fist and the blood slicked her palm.

Then she stopped. Night was drawing near. She fell to her knees, remembering herself as a child, and lay down. She looked up at the soft, darkening sky. Open and infinite unlike everything earthbound.

She got up and dusted the snow off, fetched the stroller, and pushed it back to the road.

Kept going.

Two cars drove by, one right after the other. No one she recognized. She thought about Abbe and the people who were still alive, still here. Most of them were strangers to her, but she knew they had their reasons for not being on her side, and she felt increasingly sure there was no way out.

Snot dripped from her nose, and she snorted it back in, only for it to run out again. She would be home soon.

The deserted road stretched out before her. The gloaming veiled the landscape, blurring its contours and casting them in shadow, making it all seem smaller.

In the stroller, Dream was crying.

Had she been crying long?

She wasn't sure.

She leaned over and stuck the pacifier into her mouth, but Dream spit it out. She stuck it back in and it slipped out, rolled over the bunting bag and into the snow. She picked it up and thought about licking the snowflakes off the rubber nipple, but didn't, and stuck it in Dream's mouth. When she saw that Dream was about to spit it out again, she held the pacifier in place and tapped it with her fingernail.

Dream began to suck.

She straightened up and walked on.

Salty snot ran over her upper lip. She stopped to blow her nose with her thumb and index finger, and a viscous web shot into her palm. She wiped it off in the snow. It lay there like a brand, the mark of her frailty.

THE GATE was open, as she'd left it. The house was swathed in a dark calm. Silence reigned. The black catkins made no sound as they dropped from the alders onto the frozen crust. The wind made no sound. She looked at the house, which was so very large, and thought that planning was futile.

It wasn't a question of being the smartest.

It never had been.

She lifted the stroller up the steps, unlocked the door, and parked it in the hall, letting the snow fall from the canopy onto the floor, where it would melt into pools, seep into the parquet, and discolor the wood. She carried Dream through the cold house to one of the sofas, and took out her breast. She tried to rush Dream's feeding without seeming stressed.

She laid her down on the sofa.

Dream's soft arms floated up and over her head and rested there.

In the corner of her mouth, a milk bubble. She kept her hand on the child, as if trying to push her deeper into sleep. Then she placed one of the cushions on the floor next to the sofa and ran upstairs to the closet. She took the machine rifle John had showed her how to use ages ago out of the weapons safe. She found a silencer and screwed it to the end of the barrel. She held the gun close as she made her way down the slope that led to the lake, dark and enticingly inviolable.

How long could you survive with a toddler in the woods on the far shore?

She trudged through the snow, leaving a trail in her wake. When she reached the dock, she lay down on her stomach by one of the bollards and, using it as a support for the heavy weapon, fired shots across the water. She aimed at the cliffs and trees on the other side. The bullets whined as they flew through the air; they rattled against the rocks and slipped soundlessly into the tree trunks. In the reeds, seabirds flapped their wings, rose up, and disappeared from view.

WHEN SHE woke up on the sofa, her breasts were aching to burst. It could have been morning or night. Dream whimpered and tossed her head from side to side, knocking against her. She pulled her close; the cold tip of her nose dug into her breast and the child's icy fingertips groped her skin, clawed at it. Her sucking was rhythmic and pleasant.

When she'd eased the worst of Dream's hunger, she got up with the child still at her breast and went to the kitchen. She opened the cabinets with her free hand, craning her neck and surveying the contents. Each shelf looked empty—stray tea leaves and vinegar stains—but on one there was a can of something, which she managed to open. Grabbed a spoon and devoured whatever was inside, barely pausing to chew. She kept looking and found a box of muesli that wasn't quite empty.

She opened the box and poured what was left into her mouth. The seeds and nuts had gone rancid, but she kept shaking out the contents, spilling grains down her chest, on Dream's face and hair and all over the floor.

When there was nothing left, she put the muesli box down, shook herself off, and licked her mouth clean. She scooped up the money, the CZ, and the plastic bags of ammunition from the drawer. With one hand, she unscrewed the top of Dream's bottle and rinsed it, took a few fresh pacifiers and the last carton of formula from the cabinet next to the refrigerator, and put it all in the tote bag she hadn't managed to sell. Then she stood in the middle of the room and looked at her view, swaying from side to side.

Outside, all was calm.

She was crawling with impatience.

She waited for Dream to finish feeding. Then she burped her. Through her tiny back, she felt the force of that moist puff of air.

The rifle was leaning next to the stroller by the door. She put the rifle on the stroller's canopy, collapsed it, carried it out to the car, and put them both in the trunk. Went back inside and put Dream in the car seat, strapped her in with the small seat belt, and left her in the hall.

She went upstairs, took out another bag, filled it with clothing and a Japanese paper box filled with watches and jewelry, ran into the closet to the safe, and put all the weapons in the bag too. She didn't need Abbe's help; she'd have no problem selling everything herself. Even the rifle, if she had to.

She took the hunting license out of its plastic sleeve and looked at John's picture—at his face and eyes, which were staring straight into the camera. That steady gaze.

Vulnerable but strong.

She threw the bags next to the stroller in the trunk of her car and got behind the wheel, but as soon as she started the engine, she turned it off. Climbed out of the car and up the snowy steps, now covered in her footprints, and into the house to retrieve the car seat that contained Dream, slammed the front door, not bothering to lock it, and put her in the passenger seat. Dream hadn't made a sound; she'd just sat there, forgotten in the middle of the floor, eyes wide with wonder.

As she put the car in gear, she thought about what a shame it was that this wonderful girl knew nothing of life but this. Large snowflakes sailed through the air. She started driving, but got only as far as the gate.

A white Jeep had appeared.

She backed up the driveway, parked, and shut off the car.

The Jeep stopped too.

Therese climbed out, walked up to her car, and opened the door. The snow whirled in. She was out of breath. White clouds spilled from her mouth when she leaned over.

"Are you packing?" she asked.

She pointed at the open bag at the foot of Dream's car seat, full of freezer bags of ammunition and a baby blanket that barely concealed the gun. She looked at Therese. Her eyes seemed to be gleaming, and it was like catching sight of a long-lost piece of jewelry. For a second, she wasn't sure if she could trust her own eyes, but yes, there it was: in that sparkling light everything standing between them fell away.

And that was when she decided to speak. "Are we gonna do something about this or what?"

Therese straightened and looked toward the forest. "You know it," she said. "Fuck it! It's not like I'm gonna be rewarded for staying with that dumbass."

"Right."

"Punished is more like it."

"Yeah."

She got out of the car and had the urge to hug Therese, but instead she stood in the snow and listened.

"Get this. He stashed it in two suitcases under a fucking bed at my mom's." A shiver ran through her. She composed herself and cracked a smile. "But now he's taken them to Abbe's and then he's going to bring the safe over there and lock them up."

"No way."

"Talk about being careful, right? Anyway, he'd never think I have it in me to screw him over."

As it snowed, Therese tried to light a cigarette.

She watched Therese fumble with the lighter and noticed her friend was nervous.

"But you do," she ventured.

Therese looked at her and nodded. She'd given up on lighting the cigarette, but held on to it as she gave her that look she'd missed so much, the one she'd been waiting for all this time. The look that said: It's fucked, but fuck it. We're not afraid.

She hugged her tight.

Therese's hair was cold against her face.

She let go. "I keep trying to come up with a plan," she said. "But you just have to go for it, right?"

The snow was falling all around them.

"Yes," said Therese.

B ack in the car, on the road, she warmed up and noticed she felt elated, practically giddy. What lay ahead seemed hot and exciting and beautiful. Out on the highway that feeling was subsumed by thoughts of violence and coercion. It was like flying through rooms filled with indelible darkness, darkness that had fallen over the snow and everything else. An otherworldly pall.

A plow pulled in front of her, slow as a mighty ship, lights blinking on its roof, its churning engine driving it through the snow. Icy flakes swarmed like fireflies around the low beams.

She tried to overtake it, failed, and then tried again and again. He made no effort to help her pass. Each time she glided toward the center of the road, she was met by oncoming headlights.

"Cunt," she muttered to herself.

She tried again.

Dream cried.

She didn't look her way.

WHEN SHE got out of the car, she noticed her hand had bled on the steering wheel. She carried Dream across the street to the looming brick building. A jangling came from inside her bag each time the keys knocked against the gun and ammo.

A man in gym clothes came out, his body steaming in the cold air. He held the door open for her and waited until she had gone in, as if he expected her to say thank you.

The day care didn't seem busy. Around this time, there was no yoga, no Pilates. She went inside and slipped plastic booties over her shoes.

It looked like a foster home in there.

Play mats on the floor and toys in crates. When she and Dream came in, the girl leaning on the reception desk stopped fiddling with her cell phone and greeted them brightly.

She muttered a reply.

The words seemed to come out in the wrong order.

She quickly filled out Dream's attendance card, grabbed the bottle of hand sanitizer, and smeared the gel into Dream's hands and her own. She sniffed her fingers in passing, breathing in the acrid scent until it stung. During her pregnancy, she'd loved that smell.

The girl opened the childproof gate next to the reception desk and took Dream from her, opening her eyes wide and chattering merrily in a high-pitched voice.

"It's great to see you today!"

Dream looked up at her.

"Say bye-bye to Mama!"

The girl took her little hand and waved it in her direction. Dream laughed. She waved back and lingered just long enough to watch the girl shut the gate behind her and sit on the floor with Dream in her lap, shaking a small rag doll at her, which she had fished out of the toy crate.

"Let's play!"

She could hear the girl babbling and cooing along with Dream's familiar noises until the door to the day care shut behind her. After making sure no one was watching, she headed for the exit instead of the changing rooms and the gym. You weren't allowed to leave the building while your child was being looked after, and if the child became inconsolable, the day care workers would come in and get you.

When she stepped outside, she had to catch herself from falling.

She looked down at her feet, tore off the blue booties, and tossed them onto a snowdrift.

THE SMALL park around the corner from Abbe's apartment was only a block from the gym. She followed the icy path there and waited, as they'd agreed. She thought about Therese. About what they'd do next. What she'd look like, what they'd talk about.

She felt her heart beating in her chest and a pleasing tension wound through her.

It was best to stay on her feet, she thought. The benches were covered with snow anyway. A bottle had recently been left on one of them, the glass clear, drops of liquor clinging to the inside.

She blew into her hands.

Stood on her tiptoes, sank down, and lifted up again. Waiting.

Ten minutes went by, then another ten.

She watched people walk through the pools of lamplight on the sidewalk next to the park. One streetlight brightened the ground near her feet; its glow turned the snow ochre. She'd positioned herself just outside its halo so she could observe the pedestrians without being seen.

They thought they were alone. She heard them talking on their cell phones or to each other; snatches of conversation

about what they wanted to eat, about secretaries, about strategies for holding effective meetings—incomprehensible things.
All that separated her from them was a low wrought-iron
fence and the darkness.

There she was, waiting.

An infant screamed as it rolled by in a stroller and her nip-
ples twinged.

More time passed.

Therese hadn't come, wasn't coming.

It dawned on her that this is how it goes.

Everything churning inside her was actually nothing.

Her breasts, wet with the milk that had seeped out, were
cold.

They'd start to miss her at the gym soon; they might go
into the workout room and hold up one of those signs with
the child's name on it. She had to get out of here.

She regretted coming. And trusting Therese.

When she looked up from the snow, Therese was hurrying
toward her.

"I couldn't take the car," she said. She hugged her and
smiled, adding in a low voice: "I got it into my head that he'd
start to wonder. I'm sorry."

"I have to pick up Dream in five minutes."

"Huh?"

"I told you."

She swallowed. Her temples ached. She needed to get back to the gym; she shouldn't have gotten involved with Therese in the first place.

"What'll they do if you don't show up?"

"Well, they'll probably call child services if they realize I'm not there. Not ideal."

"No, of course not. Go get her. I'll do this alone." She lowered her voice again. "The safe is still at Alex's. They haven't brought it over yet."

"Okay."

She gave her the keys to Abbe's apartment and took Dream's blanket out of her bag, wrapped it around the CZ, and handed it to Therese like a package.

"The magazine is full," she said. "But no one's home, and you're just going to get in and get out, right?"

It was as much a question as a way of convincing herself that this was how it would go down.

Therese looked right at her, nodded several times, and rummaged in her pocket. She put one of her long fingernails under her nose, sniffed, looked up at the sky and blinked. She inhaled; shrugged her shoulders and dropped them, exhaling loudly; and turned to face the icy dark.

DREAM HELD onto her hair as she carried her out. She was gripping a single lock and bouncing in time with her steps. She could see Therese coming toward them, a way off on the other side of the street, pulling a suitcase in each hand; when she caught sight of them, she started walking faster and faster until she was almost running.

Wheels rolling over snow and ice and asphalt.

Dream crying.

She put her in the car seat, moved it to the backseat, and strapped her in.

She got behind the wheel.

Therese opened the trunk and tossed one of the bags in.

She jumped into the back with the other one and slammed the door shut.

"All clear," she said. "Drive."

The area was practically deserted. She gripped the wheel and turned onto a side street and out onto the big road that led to other parts of town. Here cars crawled between the stoplights at intersections; families with toboggans and strollers waited at the crosswalks. Farther along, by the on-ramp for the bridge and the highway, the gas station's tall sign was shining like a beacon in the night.

In the rearview mirror, she saw Therese huddled against the seat, crying, one arm wrapped around Dream. And as she drove she kept glancing at them, at the shine from the streetlights streaking Therese's face. All she could see of Dream was her hand dangling out of the car seat and her hair sticking up over its cracked edge.

THE SKY glowed. It blazed and turned colors above the house. Gaping holes opened in the light, and their emptiness spread. The snow on the roof melted. There and around the windows and along the walls, everything was turning black. The blanket of snow around the house softened and shrank. Flames lapped at its edges, dispersing them, consuming them, a blue inferno.

The snow itself seemed to be burning.

The ground awakened, and all that was still alive was obliterated by the heat: pine needles, soil, ticks, and lice. The smallest of the hibernating animals.

The downstairs windows smoldered in the darkness, gusting and reeling inside. The rest were dark and mute. Smoke billowed inside and spilled from the frames.

A hissing sound. Pressure releasing.

The gate was open to the road, as Karin had left it. The car's tracks were fresh, and the reflection of the flickering fire gleamed in the pattern the wheels had made in the snow. And the flames climbed higher and higher, trying to set fire to the sky.